I0735142

A MORMON'S LOVE TURN TO HATE

Edward A. Congdon

WORKBOOK PRESS LLC
187 E Warm Springs Rd,
Suite B285, Las Vegas, NV 89119, USA
Website: https://workbookpress.com
Hotline: 1-888-818-4856
Email: admin@workbookpress.com

Ordering Information:
Quantity sales. Special discounts are available on quantity purchases by corporations, associations, and others. For details, contact the publisher at the address above.

Library of Congress Control Number:

ISBN-13: 978-1-958176-68-9 (Paperback Version)
          978-1-958176-69-6 (Digital Version)

REV DATE: 21/06/2022

This book is a fictional story.
Some small parts are taken from actual public history.
All names and charters are purely coincidental and do not have any relativity to anyone living or dead.

Preface

A Mormon's Love Turns to Hate

The year is 1885. The place is Quakertown, Pennsylvania. It was a very small town consisting of 12 dwellings, two stores, three taverns and a simple Quaker meeting house. The story begins with a family of three: the dad, John Gurney, mom, Mary, and son, Mark, aged 12 years. Dad worked in a stove and horse harness factory and mom, Mary, was a part-time preacher. Quakers were allowed to have women preachers. George Fox was founder of the Religious Society of Friends, an organization that would meet with men and women to discuss Bible study and teaching programs. Margaret Fell was a well-trained traveling teacher. The Gurney family was a very religious close-knit family. Young Mark Gurney was a loving son. Both his mom and dad were his whole life. Their neighbors, Fred and Tina Martin, had two children: a boy named Joshua, aged 12 years, and a girl named Marlyn, aged 14 years. They were very good friends with the Gurneys and lived about one half mile west of Quakertown. Mark Gurney, a young boy growing up to be a fine young man, is seeking to avenge his parent's murders.

Chapter 1

Mr. Gurney returned home from work about 5:30 PM on a very blustery and cold winter's night. He walked into the kitchen where Mary was cooking supper. He gave her a kiss on the cheek and said, "How is my beautiful wife doing?"

"I love you too, John," was her reply.

"Where is my little guy tonight?"

"He's in the bedroom laying down. He's been outside playing in the snow with the Martin boy. When he came in, he was all wet. I told him to go get out of those wet clothes and rest a while. Maybe you better go call for him, supper is almost ready."

John went in the bedroom and called for Mark, "Supper is ready."

Mark woke quickly, grabbed his dad around his neck and said, "I love you, Dad."

"I love you too, son. It's time for supper."

Quakers have always believed in silent prayers before meals; you must pray from the heart and not from the mouth.

Mary taught her son Mark how and when to pray. She was very faithful and a loyal teacher of the Book of Mormon, The Book of Latter Day Saints and the old Bible testament. Mary spent a lot her spare time doing Bible study and teaching with her friend Tina Martin. Most of all with her whole heart was devoted to her family. Back in those days, money was scarce, and bartering was the thing to do. Other than things that were given to them while out teaching, like chickens, little piglets, and sometimes a rabbit, it was necessary and common to exchange things with others to get things you both needed. John was very good at bartering to get things he wanted for Mary and son Mark.

John and Mary had three Appaloosa horses that John had acquired by bartering. He had built a small barn with a loft for hay for his horses in winter. In the summer, they could eat outside. John and Mary had about 100 acres of land. John had also built a small chicken coop with a divider to put little piglets in.

Things seemed to be going pretty well for the Gurney Family, little did they know then that within the next 5 years, Mark was going to develop some serious health problems.

Mark was a normal boy. He loved to run and race, even with the horse, but he would never take the horse without mom's or dad's permission. He felt he could never do anything to displease them. June 2nd, 1886, Mom and Mrs. Martin had made arrangements to go to a little hamlet just east of Quaker Lake, called Hall-stead, to preach to people there. So, they hitched up the horse and buggy, and off they went. It was okay to leave the children home, because teaching was always on the weekend and dads were home with the kid the Gurneys loved their animals, so they had to name each one of them. Young Mark liked to name them. For the horses he named, the male horse was Jordin, and the two female horses were Bridgette and Bernadette. Jordin was a real work horse, and the females worked good as a team; Bridgette was the only one you could ride.

One Wednesday afternoon, Mary asked Mark to go with her. "I am going to take a ride over to the Martins. Would you like to go with me?"

Mark said, "Mom, could I please stay home? Joshua and Marlyn have gone to their grandparents for a week, and there is nothing for me to do over there."

"Mark, I understand. Help me hitch Bernadette to the surrey."

After Mom had left, Mark had most of his chores done. He happened to look over by the barn fence, Bridgette wanted out. Mark went over to climb upon the fence. After he had opened the gate a little, he jumped on Bridgette's back with no saddle or harness on. Bridgette went out of the gate and headed for the near field. Mark's dog buddy followed along behind.

Mark tapped the horse with both feet, and Bridgette started running toward the outer side of the field. All of a sudden, Bridgette made a quick turn to the left and Mark went flying off Bridgette's back, landing in the grass at the edge of the field. It knocked him out cold. Mark's dog Buddy came running over to Mark and started licking Mark in the face. After a couple minutes, Mark came to, feeling a little dizzy. He got up off the ground and started walking back to the house; Bridgette and Buddy both following along behind. Mark went into the house to lie down on his bed.

John had gone to work that day to help his boss install a cooking stove for a customer, and they had finished the job in the early afternoon. When John arrived home, he noticed that Bridgette was not locked in behind the fence and didn't have a saddle or bridle. Dog Buddy was lying on the front porch and appeared to be sleeping. John just thought that Mark had forgotten to latch the gate on the fence. He went into the barn to see if Mark was there. He was not. He went in the house and did not see Mark. He checked the bedroom, and Mark was asleep on his bed. John let him sleep.

Mary arrived home at about 4:30pm. John greeted her in front of the house. "Hi, my lovely wife! Did you have a nice day?"

Mary said, "Yes, a very good day with Mrs. Martin. We had a lovely lunch and a very good Bible study time." Mary said, "Where is our son?"

John answered, "He must have been tired. He is asleep on his bed and I didn't wake him. You go ahead into the house. I will put the horse and surrey away."

Mary said, "Thank you, dear. I love you so much, only the Lord could love you more. Mary went into the house, peeked in the bedroom and saw Mark was still sleeping. She decided to let him rest until supper time. About an hour later, Mary went into the bedroom to wake Mark.

Mark said, "Okay, mom. I will be out in a few minutes"

Mark was beginning to think how he was going to tell them what happened. They will never trust me again, he thought. I wonder what kind of punishment I'm going to get. So, Mark went out of the bedroom and sat down at the table ready to say the supper prayers. Mark felt so guilty. He knew he had to tell them regardless of the punishment he may get. So, he waited until after supper and he said, "Mom, dad, I have something to tell you." And he told them the whole story.

Mom jumped up out of her chair and said, "Let me look at your head!" She found a small bump on his head. "We don't have ice, but we have very cold spring water, so I will make a cold pack to put on your head."

Mary asked Mark if he felt all right. Mark answered, "Yes, mom. I'm Okay."

His headache had gone away, but he was still wondering what punishment he was going to get. So, he waited. Nothing was said all evening by mom or dad about punishment. 8 o' clock was Mark's bedtime. Mark got up and said goodnight to his mom and dad, and gives them a kiss on the cheek. He went into the bedroom and got in his bed. He just did not understand why he was not given a punishment. He thought he'd wait until morning and ask them why. Mark said his night prayers and went to sleep.

The next morning after breakfast, Mark said, "Mom can I ask you both a question?"

They both answered yes. "What is it Mark?"

Mark replied, "I know I have committed a sin against both of you by not obeying your demands for my own safety. I am so sorry for what I have done. I am waiting for my punishment that you have not given me yet."

Mary said, "John, you answer him on this."

John said, "Mark, you have apologized this morning and we accept. This is the first time you have ever done anything in disobedience of the rules given to you. We are your parents and we love you so very much, son. We cannot punish you for a mistake you made once. And that is the end of that."

Mark was surprised but very happy he was not going to get punished for the mistake he made, although he still felt guilty about what he had done. Mark worked hard in an effort to show his mom and dad how bad he felt, and wanted to show them they could trust him.

A couple of days later, things seemed better and the family was back to living normally, except for one thing: Mark was still getting his headaches with flashbacks about every week or two. They didn't seem to last very long, and mom treated him with old fashioned remedies. They thought everything was going to be all right.

Well, in the meantime, Quakertown, located in Bucks County, was beginning to grow in population very fast from the 1800s. The Pennsylvania- Reading Railroad station opened in 1889. Land was selling at a good price and new houses were being built. The Martins had decided it was a good time to sell out and leave the area. They had relatives down in Texas and really wanted to go there. This was a big disappointment to the Gurney Family, but the Martins did sell their farm and moved to Texas in 1887.

The Gurney Family lived through the winter that year, and became disgusted with the loss of their crops that summer. The Martins had been writing to them, trying to convince them to sell and come to Texas where lots of land was available and cheap. Since they had a bad winter with Mark with his headaches, flashbacks, and winter colds, they discussed it with Mark. He agreed he wanted to go where the Martins were, and decided it may be best to get to warmer weather. Mark didn't want to go and leave the animals behind. John and Mary talked to Mark for a few days and did finally get Mark to agree with moving on with their lives. They finally put their place for sale and it was sold by fall of 1888. The Gurney family, after much discussion, did decide to sell. Quakertown village and land around the town was selling fast. A real estate investment group bought the place. The closing on the property was not to be held until spring of 1889. That allowed the Gurney family to sell their animals, and any household or other items. Mark begged them not to sell the horses; he didn't care about the two cows.

John said to Mark, "So, what are we supposed to do with the horses?"

Mark replied, "Take them with us! When we get to

Texas and get our place, we will need them."

John remarked to Mary, "Maybe he is right. We will need horses, and at least, we know our horses and how they work."

"Mary, I am going to send a letter to Fred to see if he has any room to hold our horses for a while until we get settled."

Mark said, "Dad, you want me to ask? I'm writing to Joshua now."

Dad wasn't so good at writing letters, so he said go ahead and ask in your letter. Mark agreed, but he wasn't writing to Joshua, he was writing to Marilyn instead. He kind of liked her, and she him also.

In about 2 weeks, John received a letter from Fred. He said he had room in his barn for their horses and plenty of food and water. Fred went on to say he hoped John wouldn't be upset, but there is a place about 5 miles up the road from us – real nice, good piece of land, large house, and barn. "I put $100.00 hold on it until you get here to look at it. I think you're going to like it. If you decide you want it, they will move right away."

John said, "Mary, what do you think of that?"

Mary said, "The Martins are good people. They act like relatives to us."

John and Mary's property was prime land. The investor group agreed to pay top dollar because they wanted that land for development to build houses on. They agreed payment was $150.00 per acre, plus the assessed value of the house and barn – $8,000.00 for the house, and $4,000.00 for the barn; for total sales amount of $27,000.00.

John and Mary, after the purchase agreement was signed, agreed to hold off the closing on the property until spring allowed them to sell off their cows, chickens, and pigs. John did manage to sell off everything except the horses they were going with them.

It was winter, December of 1888. Mark was 15 years old then, and was a lot of help to mom and dad doing chores like bringing in wood for the stoves, shoveling and plowing snow, and helping dad in the barn.

Mark had started drawing pictures when he was about 7 years old. John would bring home sheets of paper from work, and Mark drew something on them. Mark like to draw animals, especially his dog and favorite horse, Bridgette. Soon, it was going to be Christmas time, and it was time to go get a tree.

It was Saturday and dad didn't have to go to work that weekend. Mark and dad went to the Harvey Hill Farm to get a tree. Mary stayed home and got the decorations ready for when they arrived home.

Mary said, "John! Bring that tree in, so I can look at it."

John said, "Okay, Mary. I just have to cut off the bottom a little and mount it in the stand."

Mark said, "Yes, it's a beautiful tree, mom. Perfect shape. I have a perfect place for that tree."

That night they sang religious songs while they decorated the tree. Mark got up about 5:30a.m. Mom was getting ready to make breakfast.

Mark said, "Mom, I had a bad dream last night."

"What was it about Mark? Can you tell me?"

Mark said, "No, Mom. I can't tell you. You and dad were in it, and I didn't like it."

Mom replied, "That's okay, son. We all have bad dreams sometimes. The best thing to do is to forget about them. Maybe tonight you will have good dreams."

"Boy, I hope so, Mom!"

John came in from the barn and said, "Mary, I wish these buyers would come and pick up the animals they bought. I still have to milk the two cows, and feed the rest of the animals."

"Yes, John, but you told them they could leave them here until spring."

John said, "Yep. Goes to show how stupid I am!"

Mary and Mark both laughed with John.

Mary proceeded to make breakfast, and they all sat at the table to say their prayers, and enjoy their time together.

John asked Mark for a favor, "I milked the cows but did not take time to feed them. Can you do that?"

"Yes, I will do that right away, dad."

While Mark had gone to the barn, John asked Mary what she thought they should get him for Christmas.

Mary said, "You know how much he loves to draw pictures. See if you can get a few colored pencils, and a ream of nice white paper, and a new hat. I'm sure he would like that."

"Okay, I will stop at Sine Department Store tomorrow after work, and see what they got." Then John says, "Now, my beautiful wife; what can I get for you for Christmas?"

Mary said," I need a pair of winter boots, a warm winter coat, and hat."

John said, "You shall have them, my love, even if I have to go to Mill side or Summerville to get them!"

John told Mary not to worry about Christmas because he had enough money saved to take care of all of it.

Mary said, "Thank you, dear husband. I love you so much."

Mark comes in from the barn. John asked, "Did you clean the trough and water the animals?"

Mark replied, "Yes, I did, dad. What's next?"

"Nothing for now."

Mark goes into the bedroom to get a couple of worn and paper. Mom was busy doing up the breakfast dishes and cleaning up the kitchen. She was not paying attention to Mark. All of a sudden, there was a loud crash and Mary turned around to see what had happened. They both ran over to Mark and asked, "Are you all right? What happened?"

Mark answered, "Yes, I'm okay. Just got a little dizzy

with a quick flashback, and fell over. I'm sorry."

John said, "Don't worry about that. Tell us about this flashback. What did you see?"

Mark asked, "Dad, do you remember last month when Jordin got out of the barn and was over by the big maple tree trying to eat the leaves off the tree?"

John replied, "Yes, I remember. We had to go chase him to put him back in the stall. Never could figure out how he got out of the barn."

John helped Mark sit up, and as he did, he happened to look out of the window. And sure enough, there stood Jordin by the big maple tree trying to eat bark off the tree. John grabbed his coat and hat, and went running out the door. Jordin did not want to go back in the barn. John went in the barn and got the horse whip. He did not strike the horse, but he knew the horse was afraid of the whip. After about 15 minutes, he managed to get Jordin back in the barn and locked into the Stanchon. John went back in the house and asked Mark if he had unlatched his stanchion while he had been feeding him.

Mark answered, "No, Dad, I did not."

John said, "I just don't understand. The stanchon was open, but both barn doors were shut. So, how did he get out?"

Mary got a cold pack and put it on the back of Mark's neck to try to take the slight headache and dizziness away. She told Mark to go lie on the bed for a while. Mark did as told by his mom.

Mary went over to pick up the paper and she was shocked. She said, "Come here! I don't believe it!"

"Believe what? said John.

She showed John the picture. It was a dead ringer of Jordin standing by the maple tree trying to eat the bark off that tree. Mary knew that Mark hadn't seen the horse out there before he had drawn it or he would have told his dad.

Mary said to John, "I'm getting worried about your son, his headaches and dizziness. Maybe we better get him to a doctor pretty soon."

John replied, "Okay, Mary. Let me do a little inquiring to see who the good one for him to see is. We may have to go to Scranton if we can't find a good doctor here. Now, let's just keep track of how he is doing. Don't want anything to get out of control."

Mary said, "Yes, John. We need to keep him in our prayers every day. I don't think it's a good idea to let him ride Bridgette a couple times a week either."

"Mary, you're right. He loves to get her out of the barn and take a ride up the road to get her some exercise. But you're right. I will have a little talk with Mark about this. As much as he loves that horse, I'm sure he will agree to just take her for a walk and not try to ride her during the winter months."

Chapter 2

Quakertown had been growing in population in the past two years. The Pennsylvania and Reading Railroad was being built; tracks were being installed for the trains to come through Quakertown, and a large station house was being built, but was not to be completed and ready to open until early 1889. John was happy about that because they were taking the horses with them, and he would load them onto a rail car. John wanted so badly to find out how much it was going to cost to ship to Texas. However, because the railroad was not complete, there was no Station Master to get a price from until the station opened. It was closed for Christmas holidays.

John said to Mary, "After the first of the year, they should open. It looks like the station is nearly done."

Mary was concerned also about how much it was going to cost to ship those three horses across country to Texas after they promised Mark they would take them. John tried to assure Mary it was going to be okay. He told Mary not to worry.

"Once we close on our place, we will have $27,000.00 to work with."

Mary replied, "Yes, but we don't know what our property will cost us in Texas!"

John said, "Don't worry about that. If we find what we want, we will have a good down payment. I'm sure we can get a mortgage."

It was Christmas day. The family all got up at the same time that morning. Mark was acting a little strangely by being a little quiet. Mary noticed and asked Mark if everything was okay.

"You're a little quiet this morning."

Mark replied, "Yes, I love everything you and dad have given me for Christmas."

Mark said, "I dreamed a spark from the fireplace flew over and set our Christmas tree on fire, then burned our house down, and we had to sleep in the barn."

Mary went over to Mark and put her arm around him. She then told him that it was only a bad dream and everything is okay. "Just trust in the Lord he will take care of us." This seemed to quiet Mark down. He got out his paper and pencils to draw some pictures. Mary went into the bedroom and asked John to help her move the bed. John had just come in from the barn, and he didn't know anything about what was going on.

He replied, "Yes, wife. I have to change my clothes now anyway."

Mary told John about Mark's dream, and about how quiet he was acting and scared. She told John they had better get him to see a doctor soon.

"I don't like what's going on with him, with his bad dreams, and the flashbacks. He gets with some of them."

John said, "I have inquired around and there is a Doctor William Estes Sr. He has been the Chief of Staff of Saint Luke's Hospital since 1881. I will see if we can get an appointment soon."

John went to work the next morning, and he decided to ask his boss if he knew a good doctor that he could get to look at Mark. His boss, Clifford Buffet, told John the best he knew in that area, was Doctor Estes. John decided to stop at Doctor Estes' office to see if he could get an appointment for Mark.

Doctor Estes was in his office alone when John arrived there. He asked John to come in and tell him about his problem. John replied that the problem was with his son, Mark, aged 15 years old. John continued to explain what was going on since his fall off the horse.

"How about an appointment tomorrow at 1:30p.m?"

John replied, "Yes! My wife Mary will bring him in. Thank you, Doctor, for seeing him right away."

John hurried home to tell Mary about his stop at Doctor Estes' office, and how very impressed he felt with him. He told Mary, "Mark has an appointment at 1:30p.m. tomorrow.

Mary arrived with Mark at Doctor Estes' office that next day. Doctor Estes gave Mary some very basic forms to fill out, then takes them into his office to start examination. First, he feels around the crown of his head, then down the back of his neck, then he opens Mark's eyelids, and looks in his eyes with a scope, then in both ears. Doctors Estes sat down behind his large desk, and started to ask Mark questions about his headaches and flashbacks, and how long they last.

"Your mom says you have bad dreams. How often, and are they always bad dreams?"

Mark answered all the questions. Doctor Estes told Mark nothing to worry about for now. Doctor Estes prescribed one pain pill, and one sleeping pill each night.

One week had gone by and Mark had not had a headache, flashback, or bad dream. They were all happy to go see Doctor Estes on Friday. Doctor Estes invited them all into his office where he sat in his big chair behind his desk. They sat in front of the desk.

He said, "I am glad you are all here. I will try to explain to you just what may or may not be going on. It's very difficult to tell of a problem when it comes to an injury to the head or internal to the brain. First, I am happy to hear that he has not had any problems this week since giving him the Cannabis, but that doesn't mean it's over by a long shot." Doctor Estes continued to explain, "There could be a pinched nerve in one of the lobe areas of the brain, or there could have developed a very small tumor interfering with one section of the brain, or there could also be a problem with blood circulation to the brain. When you have a severe blow to the head, there is no exact way to treat this type of problem. I want you to continue to give Mark the Cannabis each day for now. Sometimes what happens is that this problem could heal itself and go away in time. Please let me know if he has anymore headaches, flashbacks, blackouts, or bad dreams and how often."

15th of January, 1889. Mark had not had any headaches or flashbacks or bad dreams to this date. The next appointment with Doctor Estes was the 20th of January. John had been checking every day to see if the railroad Station was open yet. A sign appeared on the entrance door. Opening day will be May 1st.

John told Mary, "We are just going to have to wait to get some information on what our cost will be to move to Texas."

Mark was doing his job by helping dad take care of the animals. Every other day, he would take the three horses, one at a time, up the road for a walk, so they would get some exercise, and to keep them from getting stiff legs.

The weather on January 19th was bitter cold, the day before Mark's appointment to the doctor. He still decided he was going to take Bridgette for her walk up the road. After they had gone about a half a mile, Bridgette was frothing at the mouth pretty heavily.

Mark took her as quickly as he could back to the barn, pulled the bridle off, then ran to the house. He opened the door and fell on the floor. Mary grabbed him by the arm.

"What's wrong, Mark?"

He answered, "Mom, I have a very bad headache and I'm cold."

Mary grabbed a large towel, placed it on a shelf in the oven to warm, and then wrapped it around Mark including his head and ears.

After about 10 minutes, Mark said, "Guess that did

it, mom. My headache is gone, and I feel okay for now."

Mark went to bed about 8:30 pm, then mom and dad about 10p.m. after reading the evening news, then checking to be sure the candles were all put out.

About 1:30 A.M. in the morning, mom and dad were woken up by Mark who had let out a very blood curdling scream. Mom jumped out of the bed, and ran over to Mark's bed. She shook him awake and asked what the matter was.

He replied, "Sorry, mom. I had another very bad dream."

Mom said, "Okay, let's talk about it. Tell me everything."

Mark sat up on his bed and told mom he was scared to go on the train after what he had seen in his dream. "The train was going fast down the track, and the horse trailer tipped over and caught fire, then the horses all burned up alive." Mark was still shaking.

Mary sat on the bed and held Mark in her arms, and talked to him until he stopped shaking. "Please, son. Get it off your mind. Try to remember it was just a dream, and railroad trains are very safe. I have never heard of a train tipping over or catching fire."

After talking to him for about half an hour, he was beginning to fall back to sleep in her arms. She laid him down gently on the bed and kissed him goodnight.

Mary talked to John the next morning. "Mark has to see Doctor Estes this afternoon at 1:30p.m. I hope he can do something to help that poor kid."

John agreed, "I will see you at the Doc's office. I

want to talk to the Doc also."

Mark was still only 15 years old, but he liked going to see Doctor Estes, and he felt he could talk freely with him, and that he may be able to find a way to help.

Time was 1:30 pm, January 20th. Appointment with Doctor Estes for Mark.

Mary told Doctor Estes about Mark's bad dream last night, and explained how afraid Mark was. "Yes, he did have a slight headache, but the flashback about the horses was so frightening that I had quite a time trying to calm him down, and get him back to sleep."

Doctor Estes told Mark to come in into the examining room because he wanted to have a look at him. Mark sat on the examining table while Doctor Estes checked all his vital signs. Everything was fine. He scoped a look into his eyes and ears. Then, he told Mark, "I am going to press with my thumb on some areas around your neck and top of your shoulders. If you feel any pain while I am doing this, tell me right away, for then, I will press behind both of your ears and on the top of your head." When finished, Mark said he had no pain. John and Mary were sitting in the waiting room until Mark and Doc came out. "I am going to prescribe a pain pill for him, but you are not to give this to him only when he says he has a headache. This is very difficult to try to establish where this problem is. I want to see him again, about the first of the month, unless he has any problems before then. Remember, keep giving him his pill each day. Do not give him a pain pill unless he complains he has a headache. I will give you another appointment for February 10th, same time."

John wanted to make Doctor Estes aware that they would be moving sometime in May to Texas. Doc said to John that they could talk about that later.

John had moved his farm machinery from behind the barn to the front of the house alongside the road. He put a "For Sale" sign on a post in front of the equipment that Mark had made for him. However, nothing happened to sell any of it for a whole month.

February was a cold month with a considerable amount of snow. On the 10th of the month, they did go see Doctor Estes to keep the appointment for Mark. Mom and dad were happy to tell the doctor that Mark had not had a headache or any problem since his last appointment. Doctor Estes checked him again and everything appeared normal. He told John and Mary if he develops any problem to let him know at once.

"I am not going to make another appointment until March 15th, same time at 1:30 P.M."

John had hired Mr. Hassle to plow the snow in the driveway, also in front of the barn. He had a John deer B model tractor. Whenever there was 8 to 10 inches of snow, he would come and plow. He only charged John $5.00 each time. The Martin family was missing the Gurney family.

Marlyn was writing to Mark about once a week, and Mom Tina was writing to Mary every week also. They were both very concerned about Mark with his health problems, especially Marlyn. She had the hots pretty badly for Mark. She was trying to show him but was too bashful to tell him. Instead, she would make little remarks like 'Oh, I miss you so much!' 'I can't wait until you get here!' 'I keep thinking about you all the time and pray for you every day.'

Mom Tina told Mary that she thinks her daughter is in love with his son. She drives me crazy because she always wants to talk about him and nothing else. Mary wrote back and told Tina she thought the reverse was true because Mark talks about her a lot also and cautioned that they would have to watch them when we get together.

February was a cold month. Everything seemed to go well with the Gurneys because Mark had no problems that month, not even a cold. John thought he had his farm equipment sold, but the farmer that was to buy it never showed up. John was somewhat disappointed. He knew he had to sell it, and have it gone before the closing on the property. Just by luck, a farmer, Mr. Jenkins from Brookdale, was passing by and stopped to look at the farm equipment.

John went out to talk to him. Mr. Jenkins asked, "How much for all of it?"

John replied, "How about $300.00?"

"Since I have to transport all of this to my farm near Brookdale," replied Mr. Jenkins, "I will make you an offer of $200.00 cash right now."

John said, "Okay! Deal. Done! It's all yours."

"Okay. I will be here next week with my large truck to pick this all up."

John was happy he got a couple hundred bucks for his old farm equipment.

Now, it was the 5th of March, and the weather was nice. The snow was melting, and temperature was in the 50-degree range during the daytime. Mark seemed to be doing well. He had not had any bad dreams, headache, or real flashbacks in the past month. He was back taking the horses for their walks, a mile every other day. Soon, the horses would be allowed out in the field behind the barn, but for now, it was too muddy to let them out.

John was still working at the horse harness factory and planned to stay there until a week before they boarded the train for Texas. Mary was not able to go out religious teaching for the church, but she did attend Sunday service. She also taught Sunday school for the children. For the past 10 days, everything was going well for the family.

Now, the date is March 15th, at 1:30 p.m. It was Mark's day to go see Doctor Estes. In the past month, Mark had no problems, and was doing so well that Doctor Estes told Mary to stop the cannabis for a week and see if he has any problems. Doctor asked Mary when they were leaving for Texas. She told him about the middle of May, but they didn't have an exact date yet.

"We have to wait for closing on our house and property."

The doctor said, "Unless Mark has a problem, I don't need to see him in April, but I do want to see him once more before you leave in May." Mary agreed.

The balance of March and April seem to fly by fast. Soon, it was the first of May, and the property investment realtors set the closing for May12th. John went down to the railroad station to see about the tickets cost to Texas. The ticket station office or waiting room was not open yet. A sign on the door said *'For tickets go to the building across the tracks called J & D Whistle Stop Building.'*

The Ticket master told John that mileage to Denison, Texas was 1,453 miles, and it takes 22 hours and 35 minutes to arrive there. "It will cost you to rent a cattle car for the trip; 75 cents per horse, per mile for total $327.06. You must load and unload the horses yourself. Tickets for the family in the sleeping car will be $40.70 each person. For three people that's $122.10. Your grand ticket total is $449.16." John had brought $ 500.00 cash with him.

"What date would you like to go?" asked the Station master.

John replied, "Let's make it for the 18th of this month."

The tickets were issued with a reminder to John: 'if there are any changes, the railroad must have a 24-hour notice or additional cost will be imposed.'

The closing on the house and property was held on the 12th of May, and they were given 30 days to vacate the property. Mr. Jenkins, who had purchased the farm machinery, did come and pick up the farm equipment like he had promised when he bought it. John notified his boss at the factory that he would leave his job on the 14th of May. He told him that the closing on his property was done. They would leave Quakertown on May 18th. John's boss, Clifford Buffet, thought the world of John since he was always to work on time, and was a really good worker. Always making sure everything was done right. On John's last day of work, Mr. Buffet gave a $100.00 bill to John to thank him for his loyalty.

The next day was Mark's last day to go see Doctor Estes, who he liked so much. Doctor Estes checked him out pretty good, and ask a lot of questions, but could find nothing wrong. He told Mary to only give him aspirin if any reoccurrence of his headaches, and no pain pills unless he has pain. "Get a doctor for Mark in Texas."

Chapter 3

Today is moving day; March 18th, 1889. The Gurney Family must be at the railroad station with the horses and equipment to load in the rail car, and lock them in within 15 minutes, then board the train themselves. The train was to leave Quakertown Station at 9:45a.m., and arrive at Denison, Texas' station called the Katy at 10:00a.m. on the 19th.

On John's last day at work, he had sold his surrey to his boss, Mr. Buffet, for $50.00. Mr. Buffet was to pick up the surrey at the rail station while they were boarding. Everything was well organized and went smoothly, until they reached the State of Maryland. The train began to slow down because there were men working on doing some repair work on the rails. Mark began to get very nervous, and started to get one of his headaches. Mary asked the porter for water and gave Mark an aspirin. She knew that the problem with Mark was his bad dream about the horses burning up on a tipped over rail car. He was shaking with fear, and had another flashback that the horses burned up in that fire. John and Mary were both talking to Mark in an effort to show him there was nothing wrong.

A few minutes after the porter had made his rounds, he came to Mark and asked, "What is your name?"

"Mark."

"My name is Junior. I just want to tell you to look out the window. Do you see those men out there with tools in their hands? They are working on some of the tracks. That is why this train is going slow. They are not working on the tracks we are on, just the set next to ours. I assure you everything is okay, Mark. We will soon pick up speed."

This helped a lot. In about a half hour, Mark's headache was gone, and he was calm. The train had reached the end of the construction area and was picking up speed. Junior was helping serve the passenger's car, when completing his job there, he went over the Gurneys table to talk with John.

"We only have one more stop, and then our final destination, the Katy at Denison. Upon arrival, I will help your wife to put your luggage on the station platform deck, while you and Mark go to the cattle car to get your horses out. There will be a yard man there to lower the gate. You must bring the horses out yourself and take them behind the station to the tie post. Do you have any questions?"

John replied that he understood. Mark was getting a little excited because he knew the Martin family would be there to greet them. He could get to sit on the back of the wagon or surrey with Marlyn.

The Martin family was a little excited also, waiting

for them to arrive. Mary waited until they were about to pull into the station, then asked John and Mark to say a short prayer for their safe arrival. The train pulled in right on time. Fred brought the surrey for the ladies, and one small hay wagon for the luggage and the men. The horses could be tied behind the hay wagon.

Leaving the railroad station, the Gurneys were very anxious to get information about their new life. Joshua and Marlyn both asked Mark where his dog buddy was. Mark replied that he had died last year. John started asking Fred a lot of questions about that area of Denison. Fred told John that the area of Grayson County was a lot like Quakertown, and is now growing fast, and so is the city of Denison. Lots of new businesses opening up and people moving down from the northern part of the United States.

"You don't have to worry, John. We are both located out in the farm away from the City of Denison. We are about five miles away to the north, and if you buy the place, I am going to show you tomorrow. You will be about three miles away from the city."

John said, "Boy! It's hot as hell down here!"

After they had traveled about a mile, Tina was ahead, and she pulled over for a couple of minutes to let Mary take off her boots, and put on a pair of slippers, and also shed the shawl she had on.

"When you look at this house tomorrow," said Tina, "I think you're going to love this place. Mary, it has three bedrooms, a nice large kitchen, and a large living room with built in fireplace."

John was very surprised when he asked Fred how

many milker he had now. Fred replied, "John, I don't have any milking cows, only beef cows. I have twenty-three beef cows right now." Fred went on to explain the money is in beef cows or cotton farms down here.

John said, "Boy! This is going to be something! I never had anything to do with farming beef cows. Know nothing about it, and less about cotton farming."

Fred answered, "Don't worry, John. I will help you get started."

John remarked, "Maybe I better see if I can get a job for a while."

John said, "I don't think that would be hard for you. We are going up past the city now, and I can show you were to go to apply for a job. With your experience, you would have a good chance at getting something to do there. The place I am talking about is T. E. Horan Harness Shop, it will be on our left as we go up the hill. It's a big place. They have a few employees. I have stopped there a few times to get wagon parts, and they are nice people to do business with."

Now, John was beginning to feel good about getting a new place to live not far from the city with the possibility of getting a job. John said, "Fred, I'm going to have a little problem. Mark's horse is Bridgette. He is not going to like me taking his horse to work every day."

Fred said, "John, let me tell you something. I bought a yearling at an auction for my son Joshua. He doesn't like that horse. It's just a little too frisky for him. You take a look at it. If you like her, you can have her for what I paid which is $100.00. Joshua named her Jenney."

Entering the city going up West Main Street, Fred pointed out the T. E. Horan. Building. "Notice the statue of the white horse standing on the top of the building?"

John remarked, "Boy, that's a big building! Do they use all that space?"

"Yes, they build buggies, carriages, and wagons. They also make horse harnesses and saddles."

"Are they expensive? I'm going to have to buy a surrey and wagon if I am going to do any farming."

"No, I don't think so. I have purchased my wagons, my surrey, and a couple of saddles and harnesses, all at a good price."

Mary was also complaining about how hot the weather was there. Tina told her they felt the same way when they arrived, but you get used to it after a while. "I know how you feel! We wondered if we were going to be able to tolerate this heat also. However, now it's livable if you protect yourself against the sun, use lotion and wear sunglasses."

Mark, Joshua, and Marlyn were riding on the back of the hay wagon. The horses they brought with them were getting a little restless. It was quite apparent they were not used to that hot weather. Joshua told Mark not to worry because once they got just outside the city, there was a place to water the horses. Mark didn't appear to be too concerned. He had Marlyn sitting beside him, telling him about where they lived, and how nice it was going to be having him live close by if his parents buy the house they were going to look at tomorrow.

They were now leaving the City of Denison. About a

half mile out was a small stream where they watered the horses. From there, it was about four and a half miles to Fred and Tina's house. Tina was telling Mary about their place, how nice it was with large rooms, 12-foot-high ceilings, three bedrooms, large kitchen and living room. Tina proceeded to tell her friend Mary that if she kept your house shut up during the morning and afternoon hours, it's not bad. It keeps the house a little cool during the day.

Mary was curious about the house they were to look at the next morning. She asked Tina to tell her about that house and the owner. Tina said, "Mary, you will love them. Glen and Gilda Moore are both 80 years old, and they want to sell out and move into the city saying they can't take care of the place anymore. It's a shame. They worked together to build that house and barn. Now, they have to give it up. They have lived there for over fifty years, and now, they are going to be living in an apartment in the city."

Mary said it sounded good. "Now tell me about the house!"

Tina answered, "It's big. A lot like our house. I'm sure if you like the layout of our house, you're going to love this house with its big rooms and high ceilings."

Mary asked about storage space. "It has a large pantry off the kitchen, with large closets in the bedrooms. It does not have a fireplace in the living room like ours. It does have a nice shelfing area for a library."

May 20th, 1889. The appointment to meet with Glen and Gilda Moore was at 10:30a.m. to look at the house and farm property had been agreed upon with the Martin family. Both families arose early that morning. After morning prayers and breakfast, Fred announced that he had bought a double-seated surrey. However, it could only hold six people, and he suggested that Joshua and Mark ride their own horses over there. Marlyn didn't like that idea because she wanted to ride with Mark on his horse. Dad told her to ride in the surrey because it will be more comfortable for her.

They arrived at the Moore's house right on time. John and Mary were very impressed with Glen and Gilda Moore; what nice people they were. Also, about their life buying that place and building, the house and barn themselves in 1849 at a cost of $7,000.00. Mary and John fell in love with the place. The house and barn were very nice and clean. John was afraid they could not afford it since he didn't know the price yet. After they had stepped aside to talk, they asked how much for this place. Glen and Gilda both spoke up to tell them that Fred and Tina had talked so much about what wonderful people they were; also, a religious and faithful family.

"We wanted someone who would take care of this place. We are going to give you people a special deal. The price is $25,000.00. We will also include our furniture and the equipment in the barn."

John and Mary were so excited they agreed to the price with everything with it. The question asked by Glen was, "Do you have the money? How fast do you want to close on this property?"

John said, "I need to get an attorney."

Glen replied, "If you would like, we could use our attorney. We can share the closing cost." John agreed. "My attorney is with Randell and Brothers. They have been in business since 1880."

John replied, "That sounds good to us."

Mr. Moore agreed to contact him to set up a closing date on the property. "Fred, I will stop by your house tomorrow to have John and Mary sign the purchase agreement that will define everything that is included in the sale of house and property. I know the attorney is going to want that before closing. On the way back home, I will stop to let John and Mary know when, where, and what time for the closing."

The Gurney family was so happy they were going to get this nice place, and even have a few dollars left to buy the needed things for the farm.

John said, "Fred! Here is your $100.00 deposit. I can't thank you enough for what you have done for us!" Love and respect for each other in both families was taught at an early age through their religious teachings and trainings.

Marlyn was 18 years old, and Mark was now 16 years old, and the feelings between them were beginning to show. Both sets of parents were aware of this, however, didn't worry about it. Because of their religious training, they both believed in no sex before marriage.

While Glen was in town waiting to see his lawyer, he took a little time to go look at an apartment. It was just what he was looking for. He knew that Gilda would love it. He gave the landlord, Mr. Dave Brian, a deposit to hold until his wife could see it. Glen saw his lawyer and presented him with a signed purchase agreement. The closing was sent for the next week on Wednesday at Glen's house, so the buyers would have one last chance to look everything over in case there were any problems. Glen was so excited about the new apartment. He wanted to hurry his way home to tell Gilda about it. He stopped at the Martins to tell them to advise the Gurney family that the closing would be next Wednesday at his house at 1 o'clock, and to bring $100.00 with them.

The Gurney family had just returned home from their shopping in the city and they missed Glen. However, were happy to hear about the closing time on the place, and were also happy to hear that Glen found an apartment that he liked, hoping Gilda would like it also. John remarked to Fred that if everything goes well, they just may be moving this weekend. Mary and Tina were busy, sorting things they were going to be taking to the new place, and making plans for their future to go out teaching again. Only one complaint, that it was so hot down there in the summer time to wear their long gowns to go teaching.

When Glen arrived home, Gilda was house cleaning. She saw Glen hurrying to get into the house. He came through the door yelling, "Gilda, honey! Where are you? I have good news! I think I have found the perfect apartment in town for us. You will love it, I know."

Gilda was happy, hearing about Glen finding a new place for them in the city. Her health was beginning to deteriorate, and she knew it wouldn't be long, and she could no longer take care of that big house. Gilda asked Glen when she can could go look at this new apartment.

Glen said, "How about tomorrow morning?"

That made her very happy because if she liked it, she could go shopping for new furniture, because everything they had was being sold to the Gurney's upon closing on the place.

Mark was concerned more about his horse and the heat. He loved that horse almost as much as he thought of Marlyn. He talked with his dad, John, about the heat's effect on the horse with the hot sun. John told Mark not to worry, and that she would be okay. "I would not take her out riding in this hot sun. Just make sure she has water, then she will be okay."

Since they had arrived in Texas, and were staying with the Martin family, Mark had had no problems with headaches, bad dreams, or flashbacks. Mom remembered that Doctor Estes had told her to find a doctor for Mark here in Texas. While discussing things with Tina about Mark's past medical history, she asked if she knew any good doctors down here.

Tina replied, "Glen and Gilda told us there is a good doctor here in Denison. His name is Doctor Daniel H. Bailey. His office is on Main Street. I would suggest that you make an appointment for Mark to go see him now before he has another attack."

Mary agreed, and thanked her. "Tina, you are so helpful to us! I thank you so much."

Chapter 4

John had borrowed one of Fred's riding horses. He had gone into Denison to look around at the T. E. Horan Building to see if he could meet the owner, and ask if they had any jobs available. Walking through the plant, he did get to meet the owner. He was able to talk to him about his past working experience. Mr. Horan was quite impressed and offered John a job as soon as he was ready to come to work.

Fred was going to go with John that morning but changed his mind because he decided he better take a ride out on his farm to check on his beef cows, and make sure they were all there and all right. He knew he had to keep track of them or someone would steal them, even with them being branded. Sure enough, two of John's large beef cattle were missing. Jack Reilly had been hired as Special Policeman in Denison in 1878. His job was to investigate all complaints with authority to arrest and confine violators for trial. Jack could also call in a U.S. Marshal if necessary.

When John had arrived home, he was so excited to tell Mary that he was offered a job at the Horan building whenever he was ready. He told her that he had a nice visit with Mr. Horan. He told him about all his work experience, and Mr. Horan appeared to be very impressed, and had offered him a job for $25.00 a week.

Mary replied, "God bless you, John! You have worked very hard all your life for your family."

John asked Mary if Fred was around. Mary said no, and told him that he was going out to the pastures to check on the cows but has not returned yet.

"How long has he been gone?"

Mary answered, "About two hours."

Just then, Fred walked in the door and said, "Hi, Mary and John! Guess what? Two of my beef cows are missing!"

"Did they jump the fence or was the fence broken?" John asked.

"No. It appears someone stole them."

John replied, "I counted all of them yesterday when I rode by there. They were all there."

Fred replied, "It must have happened last night. I saw some tracks outside the fence that were fresh."

"Has this happened before?"

Fred answered, "No, this is the first time."

"So, what do we do now?"

Fred replied, "I need to go into Denison to see the policeman. He is a special appointed policeman. His name is Jack Reilly, and was appointed in 1879. He is supposed to be a good police Officer."

John asked Fred if he could go with him. Fred said he would be glad to have John with him.

John said, "Fred, I thought this was a safe area to live down here."

Fred said, "It always has been, but as this area has grown with more people coming into the state, it's like it was in Quakertown, PA when you left. You know, John, the primary product in Texas is growing cotton. We have a lot of Mexican immigrants who have moved into this area to work in the cotton fields. Please don't misunderstand me. I'm not saying they are all bad people! But there are some that I just don't trust. It is difficult to try to communicate with most of them because they all speak Spanish as most of them can't speak English. Local farmers will hire them because they are cheap labor, and most are hard workers.

"I have to go to Denison to file a complaint this afternoon."

John told Fred he did get the job at Horan's, and was going to work the next week.

"Mary don't need me this afternoon, so I guess I will ride along with you to Denison."

"Great! We can get to meet the policeman together."

Denison was about five miles down the road from where Fred lived, so after lunch, both men took off. As they rode down the main street, they saw a sign on a small building that said Denison Police Station. They hitched their horses and went into the building.

A man sitting behind a desk said, "Can I help you fellows?"

"Yes," Fred answered. "We are looking for Jack Reilly."

"That's me. How can I help you today?"

Fred answered giving his full name and address, and said, "I'm here to file a complaint. Someone stole two beef cows from me, and I believe this happened last night sometime."

Mr. Reilly handed Fred a paper and told him to fill it out completely, then they would talk. The questions were very basic: home address, county you live in, name of road going past your house.

Policeman Jack Reilly asked the following questions, "When did you discover the cows missing? Were there any fences broken down or cut? Any vehicle or horse tracks? Where do you think the cows were taken from? Were your cattle branded? I will need a copy of the branding iron."

Fred answered all the questions and told Jack the branding iron was very simple, that it was just the Letter M inside a complete circle. Jack said he still wanted to see the branding iron. Policeman Jack Reilly told Fred and John that he would take a ride that afternoon, out to look at the field where this theft may have occurred.

"After I have looked over the area, I will stop by your house so you can show me the branding iron."

Late that afternoon, Jack Reilly took a ride out to the site where Fred had told him he felt was where the cows were taken from. Jack investigated at the site, and found that the fence wire had been cut down the whole side of the fence post. There also appeared to be footprints and truck tracks close to the fence. He followed the truck tracks down that dirt road for about a mile, then lost them. He continued down the road until he came to Glen and Gilda's house. Jack talked to Glen a Gilda, and asked if they had seen or heard any truck go past their house at night or sometime just before dark. Glen answered that they hadn't heard anything. Jack asked if they happened to see any riders go by on horses. Still, no was Glen's answer. Jack thanked them and left. He stopped by Fred's house, and looked at the branding iron, and told Fred he was going to be checking the slaughter house.

Now, it was Wednesday, time to close on the Glen and Gilda Moore's house. A hot day as it was 1:30p.m. Everyone was present for the closing. Attorney Randell read the signed purchase agreement. Everything was okay. Taxes on the property had been paid. The Gurney family was asked if they would take a last look at the property before signing. They declined. $25,000.00 cash was paid to Glen and Gilda, plus $100.00 paid in attorney fees.

Glen said, "We are moving to our apartment this afternoon. You can move in anytime including this afternoon."

John answered that they would move in the next day.

Today was the moving day. John had bought a two-seated surrey from The Horton store where he was to report to work on Monday. He hooked up his team of horses, and told Mary and Mark to put their personal belongings on the back of the surrey. Fred would bring the trunks later with his hay wagon. Mark put his saddle on his horse Bernadette to ride to the new barn. Fred came along behind with the hay wagon and the trunks that the Gurneys had brought with them, and to help John carry them into the house.

While they were busy carrying things in, John said to Fred, "I have a problem! I have to go to work on Monday, and Mark will not like it if I take his horse Bernadette. He loves that horse so much he doesn't want anyone to ride that horse. What about that horse you bought for Joshua? You said it was so frisky that he didn't like it. Would you sell it?"

Fred replied, "Yes. I believe I had told you I would sell her to you for $100.00 as what I paid for her. I know you have your own saddle, so the price is $100.00."

John agreed and paid him. "I will bring her up here to your barn today. I hope she will get along with the other horses, Fred. Her name is Jenny."

"I'll take her out this weekend to see how she does."

Mary and Tina were having a great time unpacking and placing things in the house as Mary wanted with rearranging the furniture to suit them. Everything was going well, and everybody was happy.

Mark took Bernadette into the barn, removed the saddle and blanket and put her into a stall. Then all of a sudden, he begins to get a terrible headache. He walked out the barn, passed out and fell on the ground. It was not from the heat because it was a cool day. John ran over to where he was to pick Mark up. He carried Mark into the house laid him on the couch. Mark came to, wondering what happened. Mary got a glass of cold water and gave him two cannabis pills. John asked Mark how he felt now.

Mark answered, "Okay. I'm not dizzy anymore, and I have not had any flashbacks."

John replied, "We need to get you to a doctor this afternoon. For now, you just stay on the couch and rest until we are ready to go to town."

Mary asked Fred about a Doctor. "The only one I have heard of down here is a Doctor Daniel Bailey. His office is upstairs over the store that he has an interest in or owns."

"Do you think we can get Mark in to see him today?"

"Yes, I think so. It depends how busy he is, but I'm sure he would be glad to try to help you if he can.

John waited about two hours, then went out and hitched up a team to his surrey, then told Mary and Mark to get ready to go.

John told Mark, "You are going to sit in the front seat between your Mother and myself. If you feel the least bit sick, we will stop."

The three mile trip to Denison had no problems. They found Doctor Bailey's office. He asked what the problem was. They told him the story about Mark and his treatment by Doctor Estes in Quakertown, PA. Doctor Bailey had them fill out some papers, then asked to speak only to Mark. He only wanted Mark to answer the questions. "How old are you now, Mark?"

"I'm now 16 years old," he replied.

"You have had headaches since you were 12, is that correct?"

"Yes, that's right."

"What medication have you taken to date?"

"Only one aspirin a day, and a pain pill when I get the headache."

"Do you vomit when you get the headache or after?"

Mark replied no.

Doctor Bailey continued to ask Mark questions. "Tell me about the flashbacks that you are getting. When do you get these headaches?"

Mark replied that the flashbacks always come right after the headaches begin.

"How long do they last?"

"Very quickly, then the headache gets even harder. Then, if I lie down, they will slowly go away."

"Do you have any temperature or sweating during or after this is happening?"

Mark replied no.

"Okay, Mark. I would like you to go sit in the waiting room while I have some conversation with your parents." Doctor Bailey called the parents into his office to explain to them that head trauma can be very difficult problem determining the cause. "In my conversation with your son, he tells me the only medication he has taken is one aspirin and a pain pill when he has a headache." Mary says that's true. "In talking to Mark, it appears as time went by, his headaches are becoming harder. Therefore,

I believe he is now going to be getting what is called a Migraine headache, much more severe than the common headache. I suggest we try a different kind of medicine. If you people agree, I would suggest we try starting him on a Cannabis tincture, three drops a day of which is less than a gram a day. This may or may not cure the problem, but it sure will help him. Because he is only 16 years old, I need your written permission to give this to him."

Mary and John agreed to this. Doctor Bailey gave Mary a small vial sample, and told Mary three drops a day only in a half glass of juice or water. "Now, I want to see Mark next week, or before if he has any problems. If you can't bring him to me, I will come to him but you must let me know."

Mark was not sure if he liked Doctor Bailey or not. He was very fond of Doctor Estes. Mary told Mark that he should give him a chance before he judged him.

Mark replied, "Okay, mom, whatever you say. I will go along with you because I love you and dad so much."

Just as they were leaving the village of Denison, down the road came their friends, Fred, Tina, and daughter Marlyn. They stopped their surreys. John asked where they were going.

Tina answered, "We understand that there is a college for girls Between Denison and Sherman named Mary Nash. Marlyn is interested, so we would like to get some information for her. She feels if she could pass the entrance examination she would like to continue school to become a nurse."

Mark was not too happy to hear this news because he was beginning to have strong feelings for Marlyn, and thought he would lose her if she did go to college. Marlyn, however, was falling in love with Mark, and was thinking about marriage after she finished college. They had not had an opportunity to be together long enough to discuss their future plans. Mark had never attended school since his mother had taught him from a little boy. She taught him his numbers, letters, spelling, mathematics, and calculus. There was a college in Denison named Austin College. Mark was not at all interested. He wanted to work on a farm or in a factory like his dad. He was talented working with his hands.

When they arrived home, John told Mark he would take care of the horses. "I would like you to go into the house with your mother, so she can give you your medicine for today. I think it would be a good idea if you took a little nap before supper."

Mark replied, "Okay, dad. Thanks."

John unhitched the horse Jordin from the surrey, and put the horse in the stall. He then fed the horses and went into the house. He said, "Mary, you know I am so surprised at the way that Mr. Glen had built that barn. I never noticed how light it was in the barn until I went in to put Jordin into his stall. The top of the barn has 1x2x6 inch boards in horizontal position with about an inch and a half space between the boards. I think that was pretty clever. That allows ventilation in the upper part of the barn to keep hay for animals safely stored upstairs, and it allows for air to circulate through the barn. I'm very happy the way he built that barn."

Mary had put four drops of cannabis in a half glass of water, and gave it to Mark, telling him to go lie down and rest until supper time.

John said, "Mary, I'm going to throw a saddle on my new horse Jenny to see if she is going to give me a hard time. Fred said Jenny was too much horse for Joshua. He didn't like her."

John went to the barn, puts a bridle on Jenny, then a blanket and saddle, and the horse never moved. John took her out of the stall, walked her out of the barn with no problem. He had put a double bit in her mouth in case she started to act up. John mounted the horse and started riding down the road. He had gone about a mile and Jenny started to buck. John dismounted her and walk up in front of her, and talked and petted her on the head. She seemed to calm right down. John remounted her and started back to the barn. Jenny trotted along just fine with no problem. Before he took the saddle off, he gave Jenny a carrot and a couple lumps of sugar. Then, he put her back in the stall, took off the saddle and bridle, and rubbed her down with a brush. He then went to the house.

John asked Mary if she had given Mark his medicine yet.

Mary replied, "Yes, but he didn't like the taste very well. He has got to get used to it." Mary asked John what he thought of Doctor Bailey.

"He appears to be a little harsh with his customers, but he shows a great interest in Mark's health. I guess, all we can do now is to see if the medicine has any effect. I think I will go wake Mark up now to see how he is doing."

"Go ahead," replied Mary, "supper is about ready anyway."

John woke Mark and asked him right away how he felt.

Mark answered, "Wow! I feel pretty good. Maybe after supper, I can do a drawing."

"That would be nice. Come on, supper is about ready."

Mary said, "Okay, guys, let's sit down at the table and take five minutes, and give our prayers of thank you to the Lord for our health, contentment, and food we are about to consume."

Then after a good dinner, Mark went and got his paper and pencils to draw a picture. He drew a beautiful picture of his horse Bridgette standing in front of the barn looking toward the house like she was waiting for Mark to come out and take her for a ride. Sure, Mark wanted to go for a ride because he wanted to go see Marlyn.

John could see what Mark was up to, so he told Mark, "Okay, if you want to go for a ride you can but I want you back here with the horse put away in the barn before dark. Do we have an understanding?"

"Yes, dad. Thank you. I promise I will be here before dark."

Mark was excited to get on his horse and ride down the road to see his girlfriend. When he arrived at the Martin home, he was surprised to see Marlyn sitting on the front porch waiting for him to show up. She knew that Mark was going to want to ask her about her wanting to go to college.

The first thing Mark said was, "Hi, honey! How did you make out at the college?"

Marlyn answered, "Good. I have to go Monday to

take an entrance exam to see if they will accept me. I'm glad I got through high school with good marks." Marlyn asked why Mark didn't apply at the Austin College. Mark explained he had never gone to school and that he was taught everything he knew by his mother.

Marlyn asked, "Do you have any plans for your future?"

Mark replied, "I'm going to try to get a job here in the City of Denison. Dad says he may be able to get me a job where he works."

"I think that's great, Mark. I just know you would be a good worker and do a good job no matter where you work."

"Thank you, Marlyn! I appreciate your support, and you know that I would do anything to make you happy."

Mother Tina came out on the porch to ask Mark if he would like to stay for dinner.

Mark replied, "I'm sorry, dad wants me home before dark. Thank you for asking but I really must start for home soon." Mark asked if the Martins had heard anything about their missing cows.

Tina replied, "No not really. Officer Jack Reilly stopped by yesterday and he is still checking some things out. But so far has nothing concrete to make an arrest."

Mark left for home. When he arrived, entering the barn to put his horse away, he started to get a headache. He took the saddle off Bridgette and bridle, and locked her in the stall. Mark told his mother that he had a slight headache.

"I gave you your medicine this morning before you left.

I'm not sure I can give you any more of this today. Here. I'll give you a couple of cannabis, and you go lay down for a while."

John and his new horse Jenny seemed to hit it off pretty well. He had no problem riding her or putting on her saddle. Fred had asked John how he was making out with the horse.

John told Fred, "I think the horse sensed that Joshua was afraid of her, so she acted up to see what she could get away with. I think she is a pretty smart horse."

Mary remarked that now that the house was settled, she would go spend some time with Tina to determine when they would go out teaching again and where. There was a lot of area to cover between Denison and Sherman.

John said, "I don't know, Mary. You may have to take some classes to learn how to speak Spanish. Fred tells me there are a lot of Mexicans that live in both Denison and Sherman. They are Mexican immigrants brought here to work in the cotton fields. A lot of them also work in the linseed oil factory right here in Denison."

"I am sure there must be someplace down here were they teach Spanish," replied Mary.

"Okay, when you go down this week to see Tina, ask her about this. She must know what went on here. Besides, her mother and father live here a few miles below Sherman."

Mark had fallen asleep on his bed for about an hour, then woke up and went out in the kitchen.

Mary asked, "How's the headache?"

Mark replied that it was fine now that it's gone. He felt better, so after supper he got his drawing paper, and again drew a picture of his horse standing in front of the barn. Mary asked him why he always draws a picture of his horse standing by the barn.

Mark replied, "Mom, I really don't know. Maybe it's because I love her so much."

"Okay, but why don't you try to draw something else once in a while. You are so talented with your pencils and paper. I just want to remind you of your appointment tomorrow morning at 11:30 with Doctor Bailey. You must get up early. Don't forget, it's a three-mile ride just to get to Denison"

"Okay, mom. I'm not crazy about going but I will get up early and take my medicine, and get everything ready to go. Just you and I?"

"Yes. Dad has things to do. He will not be with us this time. He is excited about starting his new job on Monday."

Mark asked, "Dad, do you think I could have a chance at getting a job there?"

John replied, "I don't know, son, since you are only sixteen years old and no type of job experience. I will talk to Mr. Horan to see if he has anything you can do."

Mary and Mark kept the appointment with Doctor Bailey that next morning. The Doctor asked how the cannabis was working, and if Mark felt any better.

Mary answered, "It seems to be helping some, Doctor."

"How do you feel, Mark?"

"Just great."

Doctor Bailey said, "Okay, I want to see him again in two weeks. If any problems, get him here to see me right away."

Chapter 5

Marlyn and her mom went to the college, so she could take her entrance examination. While Tina was waiting, she managed to talk to one of the college administrators about Spanish classes, and was told that they have started Spanish classes. They are held in the afternoon each day after regular classes have completed their day. There was no cost attached to this program, but if you would like to buy a Spanish reading book, its $3.00 for both book and dictionary. "Keep in mind that this is an all-girls college, no boys or men are allowed here. I am sure that Austin College also has a Spanish teaching program if your son or husband would like to attend."

It was Monday. John had taken his horse Jenny, and gone to work. Mary had taken Bernadette, hitched her to the surrey, and left to go shopping in Denison. She planned to stop back at the Martins later that afternoon. Mark was left home alone so he decided that he would get Bridgette out of the barn, and take her for a ride. He knew that Marlyn was at the college with her mother, so he decided to go up the road where the horses were taken from.

John's boss, Mr. Burns, had placed him in the axle and hub department to work. John was very mechanical, so it didn't matter where they put him to work. That afternoon, Mr. Horan was walking through the plant and he saw John working. He stopped to talk to John and told him he wanted him to start to work tomorrow in the horse harness department.

"We have sold a lot of harnesses lately, so I need you there with your experience."

"Okay. No problem!" John replied. "I have a question, Mr. Horan. I have a 16-year-old son. He is looking for a job, and he has no experience. Would you have anything you could give him as a job?"

Mr. Horan said, "Yes, if he is a good and dependable worker. I do need someone to clean the office and pick up around the warehouse. Send him in so I can meet him, and show him what he would have to do."

Mark had ridden about five miles up the road, then decided it was a little too hot to be out riding during the day. After resting under a shade tree for twenty minutes, he climbed upon Bridgette and returned directly home. Since he loved this horse so much, he just had to brush her and wet her down to cool her before putting her in the barn.

Mary had finished her shopping and had driven to the Martins home. Tina and Marlyn had just arrived back home from the college. Tina was so happy that Mary had stopped on her way home so she could tell her about the college, and the Spanish classes that were being taught in the evenings at no charge.

Mary said, "Okay, we can attend whenever you're

ready to start. What about our religious teaching plan?"

"Let's start next Sunday in our local area between here and Denison."

Mary was happy and left to go home, about 5 miles up the road.

John was out of work at 4p.m. He had started at 7 a.m. He arrived home at 4:45 p.m. He just couldn't wait to tell Mark he may have a job for him.

"Mark! You have to go to meet Mr. Horan any time after 9:00a.m. He wanted to meet with you because you have no experience or work record, but may hire you to clean office toilets, and pick up things in the warehouse."

Mark was so excited that he might have a job. He told him that he was going to pray every night that he would have no problems with headaches while he was working.

Mary told John about going to the woman's college in the afternoons to learn to speak Spanish, and Tina had agreed to go to classes with her. Mary asked John if there were any Mexicans working at Horan's.

John replied, "I really don't know. I just started there today. I have not met everybody that works there yet."

Mary explained to John that in time he may want to take some Spanish classes. Austin College also may have late afternoon classes, the same as Mary Nash College.

John replied, "Thank you, but no thank you. I am not at all interested in learning to speak Spanish. Let the Mexicans learn to speak English."

The next morning, Mark got out of bed at 6a.m., all excited to go to work with his dad. John told Mark he could ride in with him, but he wouldn't be able to see Mr. Horan until 9a.m.

Mark said, "That's all right, dad. It gives me a chance to see where you tie up the horses, and how you get water to them. Also, while I'm waiting, I may be able to see where you work."

Mr. Horan was good about providing a nice shady place to tie up the horses while working at his plant. He also provided water for the horses in the big watering trough next to the tie-up area. There's also a tie-up area along the other side of the trough for customers that came in to buy a new hay wagon, a surrey or just wheel parts.

Mr. Horan called Mark into his office to talk. He was surprised to see how big and strong Mark appeared to be. He asked Mark if he would be willing to work keeping the office, the restrooms, and do warehouse pickups. Mark agreed to his request and was hired. He was then shown around the plant, given a work apron, and put to work.

Afternoon deliveries came in by train each day. When there was something that Mr. Horan had ordered for the plant, it would be taken off the train and placed in a storage area. Each day at 4 p.m. One of the employees would take the company's wagon, and go to railroad station to pick up whatever arrived. If it was a heavy load, Mark would go along to assist in the pickup.

Mark was unaware that the person who was always sent every day to the railroad station and the post office was Mr. Horan's son. His name was Charles, but they all called him 'Chuckie'. Mark liked Chuckie. They seemed to get along very well together. They would sit and have lunch together, talking about their personal lives with their families.

That night, on the ride back home, John asked Mark how his first day went and if he liked what he had been given to do.

Mark replied, "Yes, dad, I liked it very much. I also like Charlie. I think we are going to be good friends."

Dad was just kidding when he said, "I don't know. Charlie is also a good looking guy. You better watch out when you introduce him to Marlyn. He may try to steal her from you!"

Mark just laughed, then said he didn't believe that.

Upon their arrival home, John said to Mark, "I will put the horses away. I know you want to get in the house to tell mom all about your first day. You go ahead. Tell mom I'm a little hungry, so I'll be right in."

Mark thanked his dad as he went running for the house. John came in the house and washed up for supper.Mary said, "Before we have our dinner, we must take a few minutes to quietly say our prayers in thankfulness for the jobs that both you men were able to get."

Marlyn started her first day at college. It was just a short day of mostly introductions and class assignments for this first semester. Her home room and first class science teacher was a Mrs. Ruth Roberson. She was tough and very strict with her students on assignments and study time while at the college. She told the students to be sure that their homework assignments are handed to their class teacher when told to do so.

Tina had gone shopping that morning in town, and was to pick up her daughter at the college at noon since it was her first day.

Marlyn was excused at exactly twelve noon. She came out, got in the surrey and said, "Let's go, mom."

Tina asked, "What is the matter? You don't look very happy."

"I don't know, mom, if I'm going to do this or not. My first teacher is Mrs. Ruth Roberson, and I have been told by some of my classmates that she is very strict and mean. I was so nervous this morning! She was stern in her voice while she was giving information to the class."

"Sometimes we all have to be stern! Perhaps she has to be that way to control some of the students in her class. I don't think it's fair to condemn her without giving her a chance. Try to be nice to her and do whatever she asks you to do. Then see what happens."

Marlyn agreed. Tina asked her daughter what classes she would have to start.

Marlyn replied, "Only three this first semester: Science, Mathematics, and World History."

Tina asked, "Tomorrow you will have to get yourself to college. Do you want to use the surrey or will you be riding?"

"You may need the surrey mom, so I think I will ride Ginger. I know it's Joshua's horse but he will let me use her."

Joshua was only 16 years old and still in school. He liked school and the athletic programs. Baseball was his favorite. He was enrolled in the Denison High School and was a senior. Next year, he would have to make a decision: would he go to college or go try to get a job like his friend Mark.

Joshua decided he had lots of time, so he would talk to his friend to secure some information from him. Unless Mark came down to their house after work to see his sister Marlyn, he would not have time to spend with him until the weekend. Mark and Joshua were best of friends, but completely differed in their likes and dislikes. Both boys had their own opinions on what they wanted to do with their lives. Joshua did not like farming or caring for cattle. Mark, like his dad, he loved farming. He was also very good working around machinery and good with his hands. Joshua could care less, but the problem was, he had no idea what he wanted to do with his life.

Mark liked his job and his boss. He also likes to travel around with Charlie to pick up supplies for the plant. Now, life was not so perfect for him because his girlfriend was full time in college, and he could only get to see her about once a week. Marlyn was attracted to Mark but could not say she was in love with him.

Tuesday was slow at the plant, so Mark was able to leave early. Dad still had to stay until 4:30. Mark was hoping that Marlyn got out of college early today also, but it didn't happen.

Mom Tina had picked Joshua up from school. He did not want to talk to Mark in front of his mother. He told

Mark he would like to discuss something with him this weekend. John left work at 4:30 to head for home. He decided to take the long way around so he could stop at Fred's house for a few minutes to see if Fred found out anything about his missing cows.

John was riding Jenny, and everything seemed to be okay until they got outside Denison. About a mile up the road, John saw two men riding slowly towards him. When they came near him, Jenny begins to act up by starting to buck and jump. John had a good hold on the harness so he let Jenny run about a half mile, then he hauled her in to stop. John dismounted and walked around the front of her and petted her on the head while talking to her. She calmed right down. John remounted Jenny to continue his ride to Fred's. John told Fred about his experience getting there. Fred asked what the men looked like.

"They were both riding Palomino horses. They looked like a couple of Mexicans."

Fred asked, "Did they do anything or say anything to you?"

John replied, "They were speaking something in Spanish, looking at me and laughing. I felt very uncomfortable."

Fred told John about a couple of places down the road towards Denison that are large farms. They own large cotton fields and hire Mexicans to pick cotton and work in the linseed factory in Denison. "We have had no problems with them yet. Why your horse acted up, I don't know. I bought that horse from an auction, not from a Mexican."

John said, "I don't understand why she acted up either when they came close to us. We have met people on the road and never had any problems with her. Like I told you once before, Jenny is a very smart animal."

Mary was a little worried. It was a little past 6 p.m., and John wasn't home yet. Mark was home waiting for dad, also to tell him about his day at work and how much he liked working with Charlie. Finally, John showed up and put his horse in the barn. He came in the house and apologized to his wife and son for being late. First, he had to tell them about the two Mexicans he met on the road on his way to Fred's.

Mark asked, "Dad, were they riding Palomino horses?"

"Yes!"

Mark then told dad and mom, "This sounds like the two guys I met on the road when I went for a ride. They did not appear very friendly and they laughed all the time when they were looking at me."

John agreed that it sounded like the same guys he met going to Fred's.

That night after supper, Mark wanted to take a ride to the Martin's to see his girlfriend Marlyn.

Mom and dad answered, "Okay, we still want you back here before dark."

Mark wanted to tell her about his job working with the owner's son, Charlie, and also to ask her how things were going at the college. Marlyn listened to Mark tell his story but did not act at all interested in his comments. Mark noticed this, so he asked her about her college. She didn't appear to be very happy and did not want to talk about it, asking Mark if they can discuss this some other time.

Mark replied, "Sure. Let's talk about something else."

She was still not much interested in talking about anything. Mark could see she was not in a good mood, so he made an excuse that he had to be home early, got on his horse, and left.

After Mark had left to go home, Tina came out on the porch, sat in her rocking chair and said to Marlyn, "I notice Mark has left already. Did you two have an argument?"

"No. It's not Mark! I just did not feel like talking. I got scolded by Mrs. Roberson today because I asked a question and I don't think I deserved it. So, I'm trying to make up my mind if I want to continue to go to this college. I can't concentrate if I'm going to be yelled at all the time!"

Tina answered Marlyn by saying, "I'm not going to ask you about what did happen. Let me say this, I know you have always been treated like gold here at home by myself and your dad because we love you so much. Now you are out in the real world and will be yelled at more than once. Please don't think I am sticking up for Mrs. Roberson. She has a tough job. But I wish you would try to be a little more patient with yourself and give her a chance. Try to be pleasant. Answer when you are asked, and ask when the time is right to ask. I must get back to the kitchen to finish cleaning our supper dishes."

Marlyn was left sitting on the porch to think about what her mother had told her. She started to cry. Fred happened to hear her crying and asked Tina what was the matter with their daughter. Tina told Fred to just leave her alone, that she is trying to handle a problem.

"Okay, I will not ask her since you know what's going on with her."

After mom had finished her kitchen cleaning, she went back out to the porch to see if her daughter was okay. Marlyn jumped up and put her arms around her mother, and they both cried.

Marlyn said, "Mom, I'm so sorry for the way I've acted! Please forgive me for not growing up!"

Mark arrives back home puts Bridgette in the barn, pulled off his saddle and bridle and went to the house.

Mom said, "Mark! You are home early. Anything wrong?"

"No. Marlyn was not in a very good mood tonight. She was not very friendly. I tried to talk to her but she was not with it. I have never seen her like this. She may have had something going on at the college... I don't know."

Mom replied, "I will be seeing Tina sometime this week to make plans for our teaching seminar outings. She may tell me all about what happened."

Mark said, "I have never seen Marlyn act like this! I hope it's not something I did."

It was not quite dark yet, but a nice moonlight nigh.

Fred was coming up the road on his horse. John went out to meet him and asked him where he was going this time of night.

"Just taking a ride to check on my cows. Hold on a minute 'till I throw a saddle on Jenny, and I'll ride along with you."

"Glad to have you with me!"

While they were riding up the road where the field that the cows were pastured in, John asked Fred, "Have you heard anything from Jack about the theft of your cows?"

"Nothing yet. The last I heard, he was checking some of the slaughterhouses to see if they might be able to help by identifying the cows by their branding mark. That's the last time I heard from him. I know it takes time and I'm sure he will get back to me when he gets any information."

Riding a little further down the road they came to the field where the cattle were. They took a few minutes and counted the cows– there were 25 of them, and they were all there in the field.

Chapter 6

Joshua was 16 years of age. Quite some difference between him and his friend Mark, who was also aged 16. Joshua was attending Denison High School. Not for the education, but more for how to get out of the work assigned to him on the farm. He was a little on the lazy side. Dad was there when he came home from school. If he complained he was tired, dad would help him out by doing some of the chores he had given Joshua. One day, a Mr. Williams unexpectedly showed up at the Martin Farm. Fred and Tina were both home. He introduced himself as the school Principal. Fred asked right away if there was something wrong.

Mr. Williams answered, "I don't know. There may be. I have come to talk to you about your son, Joshua. I have sent several notes home with Joshua asking you to contact me for a meeting. I needed to tell you that Joshua is failing in all his subjects, and will not graduate this year from High School; unless he can bring all his averages up to 80. I have asked him several times for his homework, but he will not submit it to any of the teachers and always makes excuses why not. I also have something else to discuss with you. I have received complaints from the parents of four girls that he is making advances towards them during and after class. I will be calling the girls in to my office to discuss this matter with them. If this doesn't stop, and I mean at once, I will have no choice but to expel Joshua from school."

Both Fred and Tina were so surprised and upset over this. They apologized several times to Mr. Williams. "We will make every effort to straighten this matter out," stated Fred. "Tina and I will be in touch with you every week. Please don't expel him yet until we have had time to work on this."

Joshua came home from school about 4 o' clock. He was not aware that the school principal had been there to see his parents. Fred told Joshua to go into the living room and stay.

"We need to have a talk! Your mother is very upset with you based on the things she has heard today from your school principal."

Joshua knew right then he was in trouble.

"Your mother and I want some truthful answers to some questions we have. First, I want to know what ever happened to the notes the principal gave you to bring home to us; and don't lie to us either!"

Joshua replied, "I threw them away."

"That doesn't answer my question… why?"

"I did not want you and mom to come to the school because I'm not doing very well. I have failing grades now in most studies."

"Then, why did you not come to me or mom for help?

I understand you never handed in any homework assigned to you! How did you expect to get passing marks without doing your homework? We are very disappointed in you Joshua! We also understand you have been fooling around with some of the girls in the school, and some parents are complaining about this to the principal. You are walking a very thin line, Joshua, and may even get expelled from school. The principal told us today, unless you get that average up within the next month, he is going to expel you."

Joshua was very surprised that his parents knew everything that he had been doing in the school even with the girls. He was embarrassed. His parents were very religious people and how embarrassing this must be for them. Marlyn waited until after supper, then decided it would be best to tell her parents now while Joshua was out in the barn tending to the animals.

"Mom and dad, I have something to tell you! I have a girl friend in school who has a brother in high school. She told me that her brother said that Joshua is getting himself in trouble at school. He may get expelled!"

"We know all about this now, Marlyn. Please do not discuss this with anyone else, not even with Mark. Dad has handed out some punishment to him today. We need to see if this will help to resolve this problem."

"Okay, mom. If Mark asks, I will tell him I know nothing."

"How is everything going in college? We haven't heard you say anything about it lately."

"Pretty good, mom; no problems."

"How are you and Mrs. Roberson getting along?"

"Much better! I have found out that if I keep, my mouth shut and pay strict attention to what she is saying or trying to teach, there is no problem with her!"

"What about your other classes? How are they going?"

"I don't think I am an 'A' student, but at least I have passing grades. This first semester will soon be over and my grade levels will be given out. That will tell how well I'm doing."

"Dad and I are very proud of you, daughter."

"While we are talking, I would like to tell you something, mom. I know that Mark is a good man, very faithful and loyal. I'm sure he likes me a lot or is in love with me. This is nice, but I am not in love with him! Shall I tell him?"

"No, just let him know in a nice way that it's great to have him as a friend, and that you're not looking for any commitments now."

The rest of the week was normal. Mark with no headaches or pain, he went down to the Martin's Saturday afternoon to see Joshua and Marlyn. Mark didn't know anything about Joshua's problems or his punishments. He asked Tina where he could find Joshua. She replied that he was out to the barn doing his chores. Mark went to the barn and Joshua had been doing some cleaning. He now was brushing down the horses.

Mark said, "Hi Josh! Boy, I can't believe you're out here working on a nice Saturday afternoon."

Joshua replied that he was just following orders. He did not say a thing to his friend about being in trouble in school or nothing about his dad's punishment.

"Okay, Josh. I'm going up to the house to talk to Marlyn to see how she is doing in college."

Joshua called out to Mark, "Hey! I will be through here in about a half hour. How about you and I taking a little ride down to Denison to see what's going on down there on Saturday?"

"That sounds like a good idea. Let me know when you are ready to go."

From the Martin's house to Denison was about 5 miles.

Mark was not too happy about going with Josh. He wanted to stay and spend the whole afternoon with Marlyn. Little did he know that Marlyn was also busy helping her mom Tina clean the house and do laundry. She didn't feel much like sitting there all afternoon talking about her college. Mark could see that she was not in a good mood, so he decided he would go with Joshua to Denison. Fred had just returned from Denison and told Josh that it's a bad time in Denison today, and he was not to go there.

Josh tells Mark, "It's a bad day there and I can't go."

"Okay," replied Mark, "We will make it some other time."

As he was about to leave for home, Marlyn asked Mark to stay awhile. "I am almost finished with the housework. We can then sit on the porch and visit."

That made Mark very happy. He wanted to spend the

time with Marlyn anyway. Marlyn told him, "I know you are interested in what's going on in school. Really, there is not much to tell you. I have a lot of studying and quite a bit of homework during the week. The teachers are all very nice as long as you do what you're told, including your homework." Marlyn wanted off the subject. She asked Mark, "So how are you doing at work? Any headaches lately?"

He replied, "No, nothing. I have been feeling good lately. Maybe I'm getting used to this weather. As far as my job, I love it! I work a lot with the owner's son, Charlie. He is a great guy, good sense of humor and lots of fun to be with. Guess that's why I want to be to work on time."

"What kind of work do you two guys do?"

"We have to go to the rail station to pick up orders and supplies that come in by train, work in the warehouse bringing out the leather to the cutters for the horse harnesses to be made, and bring wheel hubs out to the wheel house to be installed on the wagons and surreys being built. Then, if a customer comes in and buys a wagon to be built, many times, we are asked to deliver it for them. My dad says Mr. Horan is a nice guy. He is there at the factory all the time, and he doesn't bother anybody. He even gets someone to help you if you need it. Now, his son Charlie that I work with has a different story. He says his dad is a pain in the neck!"

Sunday morning, the Gurney family was invited down

to the Martin's for dinner. It was raining lightly that day, and John decided to take the surrey. There was room for three to sit in the seat.

Mark said, "I am not going to take Bridgette out. I will ride on the back of the surrey. We may have a thunder storm, and Bridgette gets nervous."

John said, "Okay, no problem. You would take that horse upstairs to bed with you if you could walk him up the stairs!"

Mark was so crazy over that horse. He would ride her home from work, take off his saddle and blanket, rub her all down, and make sure she had her water and food. Mom and dad knew all this about that horse. She was very gentle and smart. She would respond instantly to any command given to her.

Arriving at the Martin's, Fred came out to meet them because it was still raining steadily. He asked John if he would like to put the horses in the barn.

John answered, "No! A little rain won't hurt them. We don't have to unhook the surrey. We can walk them right into the center of the barn there, out of the rain, in case it starts to pour."

Mary was in conversation with Tina about their religious teaching program. Tina told Mary, "I really don't know just what to do. We have so many Mexican families here and they only speak Spanish. Do you have any suggestions?"

"No, but we could always go to the college at night classes to learn to speak Spanish."

"I don't think that's fair here in our country to help

them. At least they should have to go to learn how to speak English."

The rest of the day went fine, they had a nice turkey dinner with all the trimmings and a very good prayer session celebrating their years of friendship. Then, they left to go home.

Monday morning, first part of May, back to work day for the men. John got up at 5:30 a.m. since he had to be to work by 7:00 a.m. Mark did not have to be at work until 8:30 a.m. Mary always got up with John, and she would get breakfast, while John went out to get his horse Jenny ready to go to work.

"Better call Mark about 6:30, Mary. You know how he likes to sleep in sometimes."

"Yes, John; I will get him up." Mary waited until 6:30 to call Mark. He answered like he was awake. It was 7:00 a.m. before Mark finally came out of the bedroom. Mary told him his breakfast was ready.

"Do you want to eat now or get Bernadette ready to ride first?"

"Okay, mom; I will eat now."

After breakfast, Mark went out to the barn to get his horse Bernadette ready to go. Mark was not paying attention to the time. He had forgotten that he promised Charlie he would be in by 8:00 a.m. on Monday because they had a large load of supplies coming in by train that weekend. Mark ran back into the house to get his lunch, said goodbye to mom and went to work. Mark realized he was going to be late for work. However, he had promised Charlie he would be there to help go get the load coming in on the train, so he decided to take a shortcut across the field to cut off the corner to the road thinking it would save time.

John had told Mark several times never to ride a horse in a field on a gallop or a fast run, and always to drive or walk slow. Mark had forgotten all about this. He then entered the field and started his horse on a fast run. As they reached the other side of the field near the road about a mile from the plant, his horse stepped in a hole and down she went. Mark went flying over her head and landed on his back in the field. Mark jumped up and ran over to his horse. Bridgette was lying on her left side with a bad broken right leg where the bone was sticking out the back of the leg. Mark hugged Bridgette around the neck and was crying very hard. He looked up, and there stood Officer Jack Reilly.

He said to Mark, "You take my horse. Go to the factory and get your dad! I will stay with the horse."

Mark got up, still crying, and got on Jack's horse and headed for the plant. After he had ridden about a half mile, he heard a shot ring out. He knew Jack must have shot his horse. Mark went in the factory to get dad, still crying like crazy. He loved Bridgette so much.

"Dad, please help me! I am so sick, and Bridgette is dead!" He told John what had happened and he blamed himself for it all.

They rode back to the field where Officer Reilly was waiting. Mark jumped off the horse, ran over and hugged Bridgette around the neck even knowing she was dead.

Officer Reilly said, "I had to shoot her. She was having lots of pain."

John told Officer Reilly he was going to get Fred to help him remove the horse.

Reilly said, "You'd better take the boy with you, because he is having a tough time with this."

Dad had to pull Mark off Bridgette and ride double to Fred's, in order to get help to move Bridgette, and determine where they are going to bury her. Both Fred and Tina were home. John explained what had happened and Tina told Fred to hitch up the surrey so she could take Mark home, while they go do what they have to with the horse.

Fred said, "I have a skid plate. We can draw on the road that was left in the barn. If we can get her on the skid plate, we can take her where you want."

John said, "Let's take her to my place. I know that Mark will want her buried beside the barn where she always stood looking for him." They put the skid plate on the wagon, went to the field, rolled Bridgette up and onto the skid plate, then took her home.

John went in the house to ask Mark if it would be okay to bury her next to the barn.

Mark said, "Please bury her there for me." Then started crying hard.

Fred stayed and helped John dig the hole in the ground, big enough to hold Bridgette.

They rolled her off the plate and buried her. It was done. John thanked Fred for his help.

Fred told John, "I know it's going to be a rough road for Mark for a while. If you need to borrow a horse, let me know. I have all riding horses."

"Thank you, Fred, for the offer. Right now, I don't know what's going to happen. Mark is blaming himself for Bridgette's death. He loved that horse so much and has had her since he was 12 years old. You could see that horse loved him so much also."

Officer Jack Reilly had been on his way to the Martin's to see Fred about his missing cows when this accident happened. So, he did not get a chance to talk to Fred. He decided he would go first up to the Gurney's to see how Mark was doing. He was upset because Officer Reilly shot his horse. Mark just didn't understand why he had to shoot her.

Officer Jack arrived at the Gurney place just as John and Fred were coming out of the barn. He was happy to see Fred there. It saved him a trip to the Martin's. Jack first asked how Mark was doing.

John replied, "Not very well. It's going to take some time to get this out of his head."

Officer Jack answered, "I feel so bad it had to be me to shoot that horse."

"Thank you, Jack, for helping us out. We don't even have a gun! Very glad you came along when this happened. Somebody had to do it. We are glad you did. Don't be concerned. I will give Mark a little time, then tell him how important it was to put her down, and she didn't have to lie there and suffer."

Officer Jack addressed Fred, "I have been working as

much as I can, trying to get a lead on your lost cows. I have been to the large slaughterhouse and did talk to the owners. They could not help since they only handle large herds of cattle brought in by large cattle farmers. They do not check branding marks. If a farmer has one or two cows, they slaughter them themselves. I have checked at some of the farms from here at Denison down to Sherman, and have talked to several farm hands. Nobody claims to know anything. I have checked some of the branding marks on some of the cattle on some of the farms. With the owner's permission, did not find anything. Recently, I did hear of another farmer losing a few of his cows, but it's a little out of my jurisdiction. Yesterday, I sent a teletype to the office of the Texas Rangers, asking if I could have a Ranger's help for a few days. I received a reply one hour later. They agreed, and a Ranger would be in our area within the next week. I plan to take him down to the big cotton farmer because he has a lot of illegal immigrants working on his farms. The owner speaks Spanish. What we plan to do is call a meeting with myself, his employees, and the Texas Ranger. He is going to tell them if any of them are caught stealing. They will be arrested and sent back to Mexico, never to be allowed back into the State of Texas."

Mark was so depressed, still blaming himself for his horse's death. He spent a lot of time crying and trying to sleep nights. For several days, he would wake up in the middle of the night shaking, sobbing, and crying. Mary would get out of bed and go sit on his bed trying to calm him down, hoping he will fall back to sleep.

Mary got up with John in the morning started talking with him, "I am very concerned about our son. He is not doing well with this losing this horse."

"I know, Mary. What do you think we can do?"

"He is not complaining of headaches or flashbacks, but when he cries, he seems to shake all over and complains he's cold. I would like to suggest we try to get him back to see Doctor Bailey. Maybe he has some medication that would help."

John agrees. "See if you can talk to Mark. Try to convince him that Doctor Bailey may be able to give him something that would calm down his nerves and let him sleep at night."

John went to work. He was just starting his day when his boss, Mr. Horan, stopped by his booth to talk. He said, "John, I heard you have had some bad luck. If there is anything I can do to help, just let me know. Tell Mark to take as much time off as he needs. Charlie is going to miss him. He and Mark got along together great working on their assigned jobs."

Mark was now 17 years old, just having a birthday the first of May. He was 6 feet tall, well-built, and strong like his dad. He got out of bed at 11:00 a.m.

After breakfast, mom said, "We need to have a talk."

"Okay, mom, what about?" Mark had finished his breakfast, looked out the window towards the barn, then began to cry.

Mary gave him a hug, then said, "Please stop crying and calm down so we can talk. Dad and I had a little talk this morning about you not sleeping every night, and being so depressed, because you are still blaming yourself for what has happened. You must realize accidents do happen in life. For us, sometimes, it's hard to understand and not to question. We must maintain ourselves and pray every day to the Lord to help us through our problems. I can't believe your dad and I asked too much of you!"

"No, mom, you don't," answered Mark.

"I know you do not want to go back into the barn again, but what about the other horses plus other animals? They must be fed and watered too. That has been your job. Dad and I cannot do everything around here."

Mark replied, "I'm sorry, mom. Just give me a couple of days, and I will get back to doing my job."

"Dad and I want you to go see Doctor Bailey again soon. He may be able to help you with your restlessness and sleepless nights. Dad is going to stop at Doctor Bailey's office after work today to talk to him to see if he can get you an appointment. Will you go?"

Mark answered, "Yes, mom. You and dad are all I have now! I love you both so much. I will go."

John had arrived home about 6:00 p.m., walked into the house, and said, "Hi honey. Where's Mark?"

Mary replied, "I don't know. Didn't you see him outside?"

"No. I'd better go look in the barn to see if he's okay. I have an appointment tomorrow for Mark at Doctor Bailey's tomorrow at 2 o'clock. Will you be able to take him?"

"Yes. Now go see where he is!"

John went to the barn, and Mark was there. He had fed the animals except the horses. John looked at Mark, and he could see that his eyes were almost swelled shut from crying. He was hanging over Bridgette's stall crying. John told Mark to leave, go into the house, and that he will take care of this and will be in just a little while. Mark didn't want to leave, but dad finally got him to go. After supper that night, John told Mark he has a doctor's appointment tomorrow at 2:00 p.m.

"Your mother will be taking you. If you would like to stop by my workplace, the guys are all asking about you, especially that Charlie. He drives me crazy asking me about you 3 times a day, says he wants to ride up after work some night to see you. I told him to wait a couple of days, if that's okay?"

Mark didn't answer at first. After a little while, he said that he would like to see Charlie. "He is my good buddy. I loved working with him! He was so funny; he kept me laughing all the time."

"Mr. Horan told me to tell you take all the time you need. Your job is safe, and you will continue to work with Charlie. He likes you, says you're a very good worker."

Mark has another bad night with dreams about his horse, flashbacks about what had happened. Mary got up three times during the night to calm him down. Mark was unable to get back to sleep. John got up at 5 o'clock in the morning. He didn't get much sleep either.

John said to Mary during breakfast, "Boy, I hope Doctor Bailey can do something to help him. That boy is having a very tough time, and it is not helping us either by not getting any rest at night. I'm so tired. I don't even feel like going to work!"

Mary agreed. "I was up all night with him."

"Yes, I heard you talking to him!"

"Did you know he was having flashbacks again?"

John said no but that didn't surprise him. "I hope Doctor Bailey can give him some kind of knock-out pill to let him sleep."

Mark got up shortly after John had left for work. "Mom, my flashback was real bad. Last night, Bridgette was crying so hard right along with me. She wanted me to go with her to heaven. I told her I can't; that it's not my time yet."

Mary said, "You be sure to tell Doctor Bailey about this and any other things you feel."

"Okay, mom, I will. I woke up shaking again this morning."

Doctor Bailey asked Mark how he felt and if he had been having headaches lately.

"Yes, very slightly. More flashbacks than anything."

"How about pain in the head or neck?"

"No, I feel very tired and weak."

The doctor told Mary to double the medicine he is taking and give him two pills: one morning, one afternoon, then one sleeping pill, and one pain pill before bed. Doctor Bailey told Mary to give him the medicine.

"I want you to keep track of his reaction to the medicine. If he has a problem, get him back here right away. Try not to let him sleep or take long naps during the day. Give him his medicine only with cold water."

On the way home Mary asked Mark how he felt. "Would you like to stop at the Martin's on the way home?"

"Yes," replied Mark, "I would like to see how Marlyn is doing in college since I have not seen her or talk to her since before my accident."

Arriving at the Martin's, Fred and Tina were out in front of the house cleaning out around the flower beds. "Hi guys! Come on in! Would you like a cold glass of iced tea?" asked Tina.

"Thank you but we can't stay long. We were just on our way home from Doctor Bailey's for Mark's appointment, and thought we would stop to see how everybody's doing."

"Well, Joshua got a job, so that's good. He quit school because he got himself into so much trouble. So instead of getting expelled, he quit. We tried to talk to him, but he has a hard head and just won't listen. He thinks he knows it all, so he has to find out the hard way. Now, Marlyn is a different story. She works hard on her studies and is doing well in college. She just received her evaluation for her first quarter, and received straight "A's" in all her subjects."

"How did you make out today at Doctor Bailey's Mark?" asked Fred.

"Not much to tell. Just to rest. He increased my medicine and gave me pills back to take twice a day.

John went directly home after work to see how Mark made out at the Doctor's. Mary had kept Mark busy when they arrived home from the Martin's. Tina had given her some flowers to take home and plant in her own yard, and Mark was helping mom get them planted. John was so pleased to see Mark being active and helping around the yard instead of sitting in the house crying over his dead horse.

While Mark went in the house to clean up, Mary explained to John about the change in Mark's medication, hoping to get him from his state of depression and allowing him to rest and be able to sleep at night.

"Doctor Bailey told me to try to keep him awake during the day by giving him little jobs to do. By keeping him awake during the day, he may be able to sleep at night. He increased his medicine by doubling the amount at night before bedtime. I have strict orders that I am to give him the medicine not to let him take it. I need to watch to see if he has any reactions."

"Mary, on my lunch hour today, Officer Jack was riding past the plant and I got to talk to him for a little while. He tells me he has Texas Rangers coming soon into this area to continue the investigation on the missing and stolen cattle in this area. I think that's great. I hope they can find out what ever happened to Fred's cows. Officer Jack says that Fred's complaint about the missing cows is not the only one he has received. Some complaints are out of his jurisdiction, so he is happy the Rangers are coming to help with the investigation and track down the people who are doing this."

Mary told John about their stop at the Martin's on the way home from Denison. She said Mark wanted to stop to see how Joshua and Marlyn were doing, since he had not talked to them in a while. "We were surprised that Joshua had quit school."

John said, "I have not seen him, but I heard Mr. Horan hired a new man in the wagon house. It may be Joshua, I don't know. Mark could be disappointed if it was Joshua, and Mr. Horan had put him to work with Charlie."

"Oh, I hope not!" replies Mary. "That would be a shock to Mark and he doesn't need any more problems than he already has. If you find out that it is true, and it is Joshua, please don't say anything to Mark for now."

"Maybe next week I can talk Mark into coming back to work. I would have to borrow a horse off Fred until I could get Mark to have enough courage to get another horse."

That day mom managed to keep Mark going all day, so no naps. That night about 8:30 p.m., she gave him his night medicine, He went to bed about 9:00 p.m., and fell asleep in about 10 minutes. They never heard a thing out of him all night. The next morning, John gets up at 6:00 a.m.

Mary gets up with him. "Did you sleep all right, John?"

"Yes, I never heard a noise all night. Best sleep I have had in a week."

"Me too," says Mary.

"Looks like that medicine is going to work. How are you going to keep him busy today?"

"Well, I'm not quite sure. Maybe I can talk him into helping me do a little cleaning in the barn."

"Good luck!" replied John.

Mark got up about 8:00 a.m. "Mom, I had a great sleep. I never woke up all night! I feel great!"

"Okay, time for a good breakfast!"

Chapter 7

About a week had gone by since the accident with Mark's horse. Mark was still having a difficult time with it, still blaming himself for the whole thing, and missing his Bridgette so much. It was so hard trying to control his emotions.

Mary and John tried to help him by giving him some information out of the Bible about death and praying every day for his help. Mark was taught by his mom from a little boy to pray and talk to God. Mark did build enough courage to go into the barn and do his chores like dad had asked him to do. John had been talking to Mark trying to get him to agree to go with him to look at some horses.

"Son, you need to get another horse! Soon you will be going back to work. How are you going to get there? It was hard for Mark to understand dad was not trying to replace Bridgette.

The Martin's came for Sunday dinner. Tina told Mary she had received a letter from Margaret Fell.

"She is coming here next week, and wants to meet with us to help us get our teaching program off and running in this area!"

Fred talked to John and Mark about a big horse auction coming up that weekend. Fred asked John and Mark if they would go to this horse auction.

Mark said, "If you and dad go with me, I will consider going."

"Okay, please let me know by Friday. You know it's down in Sherman, so we will have to leave here by 7:30 a.m. The auction starts at 10:00 a.m. Have you got money?"

"Yes," replied Mark. "I saved some money while I was working."

Fred replied, "Well, that's good because this is a cash only auction."

Joshua and Marlyn did not come with them but did show up later that afternoon. Mark was so happy that he would get to see Marlyn for the afternoon, and also get to talk to Joshua about his job at the factory. Tina and Mary were working together in the kitchen getting a supper meal together. While talking about their families and the current events going on, the kids were out sitting on the front porch visiting.

John and Fred walked down to the barn to feed, water, and look at the horses. John had asked Mark to clean up around Bridgette's stall, which he did.

John was telling Fred about the problems they were having with Mark over the loss of that horse. How he is blaming himself for what happened. Also, the sleepless nights and the new medicine Doc put him on, and that they were for the best.

Fred said, "If we can get him to buy a horse, this may

help a lot!"

"Thank you, Fred, for helping me talk to him about buying a horse."

Mark was sitting on the porch waiting for Joshua and Marlyn to show up. It was about 2:30 p.m., and down the road they came. They tied the horses by the barn and walked up on the porch, then sat down by Mark. They were both aware of how depressed Mark was over the loss of his horse, so avoided talking about it. Joshua started the conversation, telling Mark he had quit school and gotten a job at Horan's.

Mark then asked, "Well, where do you work there?"

Joshua replied, "They put me in the hub and wheel shop. Then, I have to go out with Charlie to pick up supplies at the railroad station three times a week. That used to be your job, right Mark? Charlie is always asking about you, wanting to know when you are coming back to work. He misses you too, told me you were a damn hard worker."

Mark then turned to Marlyn and asked her how everything was going at college Marlyn answered that everything is just fine. Mark noticed Marlyn was kind of quiet, so in an effort to get her to talk, he asked about her subjects and were they hard.

Marlyn again answered, "No, if you're willing to study, there's nothing to it." Then, she speaks up and excuses herself. "I have to go see mom about something."

Marlyn went into the house. Mom was in the kitchen doing dishes. Marlyn asked, "Mom? Can I ask you a question?"

"Sure, what is it?"

Marlyn replied, "I just don't know what to do with this situation with Mark. I can tell by the way he talks and the questions he asks about our friendship like are we still okay. What he means is am I in love with him. Mark is a nice guy and always has been a gentleman. Our friendship started when we were kids. I like Mark a lot, but I do not love him. So, should I get together with him and tell him there is no love for him? What do you think I should do? I don't want to hurt his feelings."

Mom said to Marlyn, "I do understand what you are talking about. Please listen to me for a minute. Mark has had some rough times lately. He lost his horse that he loved so much. Now, he thinks he is losing you and Josh as friends. What I would suggest is this, talk and treat him gently like your old friendship was. Give him some time to adjust. Keep saying your prayers for him, and the Lord will provide a way for you both and he will understand."

When leaving to go home, Fred told Mark, "I will be here 7:30 in the morning. We will put your saddle and blanket on the back of the surrey. If you buy a horse at the auction, you can ride her home. Please be up and ready to go."

"Okay," replied Mark.

The next morning was a nice bright sunny day. They arrived just before the city of Sherman at the farm auction barn. It was 10:00 a.m. Because this was a known auction barn, the yard was all fenced in and many horses where roaming around in the area. There was a podium built in front of the barn doors, large enough to hold ten people.

A man stepped up to the podium. "My name is Earl Chapman, and I will be your auctioneer today. I want to inform you all that this is a cash only auction. Here, beside the podium, are number cards. Please take one. When you bid, hold that card up so I can see it. If you are awarded a bid, the two ladies standing here beside me will take your money. Bring your harnesses up to pay and take your horse. They will be brought to the gate."

Mark was standing next to the fenced-in area, with his arm lying on the top of the fence. Suddenly, a Palomino horse walked over and laid his head on top of Mark's arm. Mark turned and petted the horse. After a while he said, "Dad, I like that Palomino."

"Okay," replied John. "We will bid on him when it comes up."

John walked over and pulled off a bid number for Mark.

Mark said, "I don't know how to do this. You bid for me, dad. Only on that Palomino when it comes up for bid."

The auction bidding started right on time. First, a couple of team horses were sold. Then, they started bids on riding horses that were already broken to ride. Then put up for sale three horses were sold ahead of the palominos.

The auctioneer announced, "Next horse is a two-year-old Palomino. Now open for bids! Do I hear $75.00? Number 12 bids $75.00."

Mark's number was 15. John held up his card and bid $95.00.

"I have $95.00," said the auctioneer. "Do I hear $100.00? Number 12 bids $100.00. Do I hear $125.00? Number 15 bids $125.00. 20 bids $135.00. Do I hear $150.00? Number 12 bids $150.00. Do I hear $175.00?"

John holds up the number 15 and bids $200.00.

"I have $200.00. Do I hear any more bids? $200.00 going once, $200.00 going twice, $200.00 going three times. Bidding closed sold to Number 15."

John and Mark went down to pay cash and pick up the horse. The horse walked right over to Mark. He petted him on the head.

John said, "What are you going to name him?"

Mark replied, "Did you see the diamond shaped star between his eyes? His name will be Diamond."

"Sounds good, Mark. Let's go home."

Fred brought the surrey over where John and Mark where standing with the horse. Mark took the blanket and saddle off the back of the surrey. He put the blanket on Diamond's back. The horse did not move, so he picked up the saddle and put that on Diamond's back, and he still did not move. Mark pulled tight the belly strap on the saddle, then walked around in front of Diamond, petted him on the head and pulled a couple of carrots out of his pocket and gave them to Diamond.

"Well, so far so good," remarked Fred. "Now see if you can ride him."

Mark then slowly got up in the saddle. Diamond did not move. Mark said, "Giddy up!", and Diamond started walking around.

John said it looked like the horse that Mark liked, and Fred agreed. John unhooked his horse, Jenny, from behind the surrey so he could ride home with Mark. Fred said he would see them tomorrow for dinner.

Mark and John headed for home on a nice slow gallop. Mark was a little skittish of Diamond for a while, afraid he would all of a sudden act up, but it didn't happen. Arriving home, Mark told dad that he would put the horses in the barn. Mary was waiting to see what kind of horse Mark got. John told her a 2-year old Palomino.

"I think he is going to love this horse a lot, he is a beauty. Mark named him Diamond. He has a small Diamond shape on his forehead between the eyes."

Mary asked, "Did Mark pay for the horse or did you buy him?"

John answered, "No. Mark paid $200.00, and took the money out of his own pocket. He had saved this money from working. I think he was going to spend some of it on Marlyn, but now, most of it is gone. He will have to wait until he gets some paychecks."

Mark had put the horses in the barn and pulled off the saddles, blankets, and bridles. He came running into the house to tell his mom about the new horse.

"You know, mom, I think Diamond is like Bernadette. He kept leaning sideways wanting to get in the stanchion next to her."

"So, what did you do?"

"I put her there. She seemed okay with him being beside her. Hope they don't try to bite each other."

John spoke up and said, "Just leave them alone. They will adjust to each other."

The next day was Sunday, and Mark knew the Martin's were coming for dinner. He was excited because he wanted to show Marlyn his new horse, and of course, her brother Joshua, because he would be riding Diamond to work the next day.

Sunday was also a day of worship, either in the church or outside. The Martin's, upon arrival, had a surprise with them. Margaret Fell, the preacher and religious teacher, had arrived Friday and come to stay for a week to help Mary and Tina. She had been invited to do so before she left Quakertown.

All family members were asked to come in the house to the large dining room for a pray service provided by Margaret Fell. Her religious sermon lasted about an hour and a half. There was no Jehovah's Witness or Kingdom Hall Church built in that area yet. When the service was over, John asked Fred if he had heard anything about the Texas Rangers coming there anytime soon.

Fred replied, "Yes, in fact two Rangers are supposed to arrive here sometime this week. I need to take a ride to the field and count my cattle to see if I have any missing this time."

John got Jenny out of the barn and Mark asked if he could ride along. Fred said, "Sure! I'd like to see your new horse anyway. I hear he's a beauty."

The only reason that Mark wanted to go with him, was that Marlyn hadn't come with the family that day to dinner, claiming she had too much home work to get done for school.

Fred suggested that they watch along the fence line for

broken or cut wires. They approached the field where the cattle were housed. Arriving at the gate to the field, Fred and John entered to go to the wooded area to see if they could count the number of cows that Fred had pastured there. Mark refused to take Diamond into the field, so he stayed out by the fence gate. He still could not get over what had happened to Bernadette. It was going to take a while to get used to Diamond.

Now Fred had built up his herd of cattle to thirty-four in number. As John and Fred search the wooded area, they only found thirty-three heads.

Fred said to John, "You go along the north fence line and I will travel the south end line. Look for breaks in the fence. We will meet back at the main gate."

Both men found the fences secure. "Well," said Fred, "looks like I have another one missing."

John remarked to Fred, "Looks like you have had three cows missing in the middle of this month and a half. I hope when the Texas Rangers get here, they can get a good lead on this and find out who is stealing your cattle."

"Officer Jack Reilly stopped by the house about 7:00 p.m. on Thursday to tell me that the Rangers will be here by Monday or Tuesday."

Marlyn was doing well in her college with her subjects and extracurricular activities. One day, while off from college, Marlyn went shopping with her mother. She asked mom to drop her off at Theodore Reber Bookstore in Denison. That's where she met Charlie Horan. He was there also looking for a reference book for his college classes at Austin College. They both looked at each other and liked what they saw.

Charlie walked over to Marlyn and said, "May I introduce myself? My name is Charlie Horan. And you are?"

She replied, "Marlyn Martin. Nice to meet you."

Marlyn was impressed with Charlie. He was a nice looking guy with a nice smile and very polite.

Charlie asked Marlyn, "Do you live around here? I haven't seen you here before."

"Yes, I live with my parents on a farm on Denison Road. My dad is a cattle farmer and I am a college student attending Mary Nash All-Girls School."

Charlie replied, "I also attend college afternoons and evenings at Austin for Men-Only College. During the day, I work for my dad in his factory."

Marlyn asked, "Are you related to the T.E. Horan that has the big factory on the hill?"

"Yes, that is my dad's factory."

Marlyn asked Charlie what course of study he was doing.

Charlie replied, "Accounting and business management. How about you?"

Marlyn replied, "Sociology and mental health programs."

"That sounds interesting. Good Luck. It was so nice to talk to you. Hope to see you again sometime! Have a good day."

"Thank you," replied Marlyn. She looked out the window and her mother was sitting in the surrey just waiting for her. Marlyn picked up her notebook and ran out the door to the surrey, a little excited wanting to tell her mom who she had met. "Mom! I bet you can't guess who I met in the Library."

Mom said, "I saw a young man come running out the door. He mounted his horse and left."

"Do you know who he is?"

"No, I do not."

"His name is Charlie Horan, and his dad owns the big factory on the hill where Mr. Gurney, Mark and Joshua all work. We will talk about it on the way home."

"Well, let me ask you a question. How do you feel about meeting Charlie?"

"He seems so nice, mom! He's in college also. I want to get to know him better."

"Okay, but just be careful until you find out what kind of guy he really is."

Monday morning, John heads to work 6:30 a.m. Mark wouldn't have to be in until 8:00 a.m. He was excited about getting back to work. After breakfast, he went to the barn. He got Diamond outside, put the saddle on, and headed for work. He was so excited to see Charlie and to go to the rail station with him to pick up the supplies. Little did he know he was in for a surprise that day.

Charlie was happy to see Mark back to work. He said to Mark, "We have a load of supplies to be picked up today at the railroad station. Will you go with me? Josh doesn't want to go."

"Yes, I will go with you anytime, Charlie, you know that. I always thought that was part of my job here."

Charlie tells Mark he thinks that Josh is a little on the lazy side and that he will try to get out of work wherever he can. The supplies were to be picked up after 1:30 p.m. when the train arrived at the station. In the meantime, Mark was working in the wheel and hub shop where his dad was working that day. Mark did not see Josh anywhere. He was supposed to be working in supply receiving department.

On the way to the railroad station, Charlie told Mark, "Guess what, buddy? I met a new girl last week at the library. She was very nice. I think she liked me too. I'm hoping to see her again sometime this week. She is also a college student."

Mark asked her name.

Charlie said "Marlyn is all I got."

Mark replied, "That's nice. I wish you good luck." He suspected it might be Miss Martin, but he said nothing to Charlie.

John and Mark both left work at the same time, 4:00 p.m. so they could ride home together. Mark was kind of quiet. He acted like he didn't want to talk.

John became a little concerned and asked Mark, "Do you have a headache?"

Mark replied, "No, dad, I'm Okay."

John said, "You're very quiet. Did something happen at work?"

"No, dad. Everything is okay." He did not want to tell him he had Marlyn on his mind after what Charlie had told him about meeting a girl. Mark asked, "Dad, can we stop at the Martin's on the way home?"

"What for? They were just at our house yesterday. I see no reason to stop there tonight."

"Oh, I just wanted to see if Joshua was home. I didn't see him at work today. He was to be in the receiving department to help us unload the supplies, but when we came in, he was not there. Charlie was looking for him also. He says that Joshua is a little lazy and may do his best to get out of work when he can, especially when it is something he doesn't like to do. He may wind up getting fired soon."

Nothing more was said between the two until they arrived home. Mark offered to put the horses away. Then, he wanted to get in the house to talk to his mom about Marlyn, to see if anything was said Sunday about meeting Charlie.

Mark decided he would do his chores before he went into the house to talk to his mom about Marlyn. He was thinking maybe it was not Marlyn Martin, but another girl named Marlyn. *How stupid I was! I should have asked Charlie to see if he could get her last name.* Now, Mark had brushed down his horse and fed the animals, chickens, and a couple of piglets John had bought. No cows. By that time, it was about 6:00 p.m. so he went in the house for supper.

Mary was busy in the kitchen, preparing supper. Dad John was sitting at the table reading the paper. Mark knew that was not the time to talk to mom, so he would wait until after supper when dad left the room. He didn't want dad to know he wanted to talk to mom about Marlyn. Mark sometimes helped his mom with the supper dishes, and they could talk while they were working. Dad like to go sit in the living room to read.

Mark said, "Mom, I need to ask you a question. When the Martin's were here yesterday, did Marlyn say anything to you about meeting a guy named Charlie?"

"No, why do you ask?"

"I just wondered. I work with a guy named Charlie, the boss's son. So, does she have a boyfriend?"

"No, Mark. Nothing was said while they were here."

Chapter 8

The day was Tuesday, 1890. Two Texas Rangers showed up in the City of Denison, Texas. They were not dressed in Ranger outfits, just their own clothes. Most people would not know who they were. They stopped at Officer Jack Reilly's office. Texas Ranger number one introduced himself as Captain Bob Chower. The Second Ranger introduced himself as Stephan F. Austin. He was a Spanish-speaking Ranger. Officer Jack was so happy to meet them and discuss the many problems he was having in the City of Denison, and outside the city with horses and cows both being stolen from various locations in and around town.

Officer Jack spent about an hour filling the Rangers in on what was going on in that area. The Rangers asked Officer Jack to take them tomorrow afternoon to meet and talk to the Martin and Gurney families, because they needed to get statements from both of them. Officer Jack had assured them he would be ready to escort them to meet with both families.

That night, Officer Jack rode out to the Martin's house to inform them to be home tomorrow since the Texas

Rangers would be in town, and it would be important they give statements.

On Wednesday morning, the Rangers stopped at Officer Reilly's office. He was to go with them to show them where the Martins lived, then stop at the Gurney's on their way to the field where the cows were taken from so the Rangers could inspect the land area and fencing around that field.

Arriving at the Martin's home about 8:30 a.m., Fred invited them in the house for coffee. The Rangers thanked him but said that they had to take a statement before we can start their investigation.

"Primary information has been given to us by Officer Reilly on your first complaint, but we understand, you now have another cow missing. How many heads of cattle do you currently own?" asked Captain Bob Chower.

"Thirty-five"

"Did you buy the calves from a farmer or a cattle broker?"

Martin replied, "A cattle broker."

"Who branded them?"

"The broker," replied Martin. "I had to have the branding iron made before they would brand them after purchase."

Captain Chower asked, "All cattle you own have been branded?"

"Yes."

"Name of the broker?" asked Chower.

"H. Smith Broker and Branding cattle."

The Rangers thanked Mr. Martin for his statements and left to go look to the field where the cows were. When the Rangers arrived at the fenced area where the cattle were kept, they noticed the fence seemed to all be in good condition and intact right up to the gate entrance. Ranger Stephan Austin dismounted his horse to examine the gate and found the fence had been cut on the back side towards the field. Then, small strands of wire were used to pull the wire and fasten it to the back side of the gate, now making it appear it had never been opened. The Rangers told Officer Jack that they had seen fenced gates cut the same as this gate was cut. They looked for clues inside and outside the gate, but found nothing but hoof prints from horses that had been there before.

On the way back to Dennison, they wanted to stop at the Horan Factory and talk to Mr. Gurney to see if he had any information that would help. John Gurney could only give them basic information that Martin had given them. However, he did tell the Rangers about the two strange-acting Mexicans that he and his son had met on the road on their way home from work.

The next day, it didn't take long for the word to spread around Denison that there were two Texas Rangers in town. People were wondering why. They must be looking for someone. The Texas Rangers had quite a reputation of being a very rough and tough organization, in their effort to uphold the laws of the State of Texas. From 1894 to 1898, the Rangers scouted 173,391 miles, made 676 arrests, and returned 2,856 head of stolen livestock to their owners. Along the way, they were challenged by outlaws and crooks. But they soon found out you don't mess with the Rangers. They were very well trained in the use of firearms and fast to respond to any challenging situation. Crime in the two cities of Denison or Sherman was not high, but it was not uncommon for gangs like the Willie Pasco gang to come into the city for a couple of days. They visited the local bars and the prostitutes, then left. Once in a while, a robbery if they saw something they wanted.

Officer Reilly was asked many times by the residents if the Rangers were there chasing the Pasco gang members. Officer Reilly claimed to know nothing. The Texas Rangers had the authority to make arrests anywhere in the state. They decided first of all to scout out Grayson County to see the area where the crimes may have been committed.

That morning, they talked to Officer Reilly and asked who was a big rancher in the area that might hire slaves and Mexicans. Officer Reilly gave them information about a cotton farmer, not far from there.

"His name was Benjamin Franklin Colbert, and he owned about twenty-five slaves, which most of them were negroes." He wasn't sure if Colbert had any Mexicans working there or not.

"What kind of a guy is he? Do you think he would let us talk to his workers? Does he know you?"

Reilly answered, "Yes."

"Can you set up a meeting for us to talk?"

"Yes, I could."

The next day, Officer Reilly had set up a meeting for the Rangers with Mr. Colbert and approved to have his employees at 7:00 p.m. be there by the house, and let the Rangers talk to all of them. There were about fifty employees including the twenty-five slaves, gathered for the meeting.

The next night, about twenty-five were Mexican immigrants with no work papers. Mr. Colbert was first to address his employees by introducing the Texas Ranger, Stephan F. Austin, who spoke Spanish and English.

As he addressed the crowd, told them his name again and said, "We are here investigating the theft of some beef cattle in this area. If you know anything about this, better tell us now, because if we find out you did know or were part of this, we will arrest you and put you in jail. You could spend considerable time there waiting for the circuit judge to come to this area and still spend more time in jail, plus pay for the cows."

When Ranger Austin had finished his speech, Mr. Colbert also addressed the workers saying, "If I find out this is true, I will fire you and never rehire you again. Now, if you know something, I want you to come to me first. I will go with you to report what you know to the Rangers. Many of you have worked faithfully for me for the past few years. I would not like to see that end, so please cooperate if you know anything."

The Rangers thanked Mr. Colbert for his cooperation and left. Texas Ranger Captain Bob Chower wanted to know who, as a police Officer, was in charge in Sherman, eight miles down the road from Denison. Officer Reilly told him the man to see was Officer James Lee Hall. He was a school teacher who wanted to be in law enforcement and had become City Marshal in Sherman. He was a good officer and a hard worker at that. Officer Chower asked Officer Reilly if he had contacted him about the missing cattle. Officer Reilly told the Rangers that he had met with Officer Hall, and did discuss the whole problem concerning the missing cattle and other criminal activities. Officer Hall said that he also had had several complaints of missing cattle in his area also, and has been trying to investigate this matter without success so far. Captain Chower wanted to set up a meeting with Officer Reilly and Hall to compare information they both had obtained in their investigations to date. This was arranged by Officer Reilly.

The meeting was held in Officer Hall's office while Ranger Austin covered at Officer Reilly's office. It was discovered that there were about fifty head of cattle stolen or missing so far in Grayson County alone. After much discussion, plans where to be made for further investigations.

Chapter 9

Mark had been doing pretty well lately, getting along good on his job, learning a lot about mechanics, and how to assemble buggies, surreys, wheel carts, and wagons. Like his dad, he made sure to get up in the morning early to be sure to get to work on time. He loved his horse Diamond so much with his whole heart, like he loved his parents. He did not want to take any chances with that horse.

Mark and Charlie had become very good friends and worked well together. Little did Mark know that Charlie and Marlyn were becoming close friends by their meeting at the library twice a week and discussing their college programs. Mark was a little annoyed he didn't see much of Marlyn anymore because she was always working on her college studies.

One day, Charlie and Mark went to pick up supplies at the rail station, and Charlie said to Mark, "I think I'm falling in love with this girl Marlyn."

Mark asked, "What's her last name?"

"Martin. Do you know her?"

Mark was so surprised that he answered yes. Now,

he felt hurt that Marlyn had said nothing to him, when she knew he cared so much for her. When Charlie tried to question Mark about her, he said she was only a neighbor, that's how he knew her as a kid.

John and Mark left work that night at 4:30 p.m. John noticed Mark was very quiet and acted like he didn't want to talk. John asked Mark if he was okay.

"You're very quiet tonight."

Mark replied that he was okay. He had not had one of his headaches lately, so dad was a little concerned. Dad knew nothing of what had gone on between Mark and Charlie. Mark was not ready to talk about that conversation.

Upon arrival home, John told Mark to go in the house, see mom and try to rest a little before supper. He would put the horses away.

When John came in from the barn, Mary asked, "Is everything okay with you and Mark? He seemed quiet and said he was going to lie down for a while, and to call him when supper was ready. He did not walk over and give me a kiss like he always does."

"I don't know, Mary. I asked him if he was okay and he replied yes but didn't want to talk."

"Well, maybe he is tired from a long day. Let him rest for a while."

Supper was ready. Mary went to the bedroom and gently woke up Mark. Then again, she asked him if he felt okay.

Mark answered, "Yes, mom. I'm okay. Don't worry about me."

"Well, supper is ready; come and eat."

The three of them sat at the kitchen table and quietly said their prayers. After supper, Mark always helps mom to clear the table and do the dishes, but he made no attempt to help her that night. Instead, he went to the bedroom and came out with a handful of colored pencils and a regular sheet of white paper. John and Mary never said a word but just sat down to talk to each other about their day, and watched Mark sitting at the table doing pencil sketches. Mary happened later to walk past the table and saw that Mark had drawn a beautiful picture of a lady in a wedding dress.

Mary remarked to Mark, "Boy, what a beautiful picture! That looks just like Marlyn."

Again, Mark didn't answer her question or make any remarks, but was sober-faced. He got up from the table took his drawing, kissed Mom and Dad, and said his goodnight. He left and went to his bedroom.

Mary asked John, "Did something happen at work that Mark is not telling us about? He is acting very strange."

"I know," replied John. "He didn't say two words to me on the way home. Everybody at work seems to like Mark a lot. He's always ready to jump in and help any of the guys that may be having trouble. I can't understand what is happening. He doesn't seem to want to tell us about it."

During the night, Mark let out a scream of pain. Mary and John jumped out of bed and ran over to him.

"Are you having pain?" asked Mary.

"Yes!"

"You lie quite as you can. I will get you some of your medicine and a cold wash cloth." Mary went to the kitchen cupboard, got Mark's medicine, and then gently rubbed the back of his neck. She knew this was not the time to ask questions. Mark settled down after a couple of hours and fell asleep. However, Mary and John were up all night, not knowing what would happen next.

That morning, John told Mary, "I'm going to lie down for a couple of hours. Call me at noon, then I may go into work. I know Mark's not going to be able to go today."

Mary went to the bedroom to check on Mark. He was awake still having a little headache. Mary told Mark it was time for his medicine again. "Have you had any flashbacks?"

"None so far, mom."

"When you're up and feeling better, I think it might be time to make an appointment to see Doctor Bailey. Besides, you are getting low on your medicine."

John got up at noon and decided he was going in to work, hoping if he asked around, he might be able to find out what caused Mark's state of mind and what was bothering him. The first one he met entering the factory was Charlie. He asked John where his buddy Mark was. John told Charlie that Mark was sick with headaches.

John asked Charlie, "Do you know if Mark had any problems with anyone here in the factory? He seems very depressed and don't want to talk about it."

Charlie answered, "Gee, I don't know. He was fine working with me yesterday when we went to pick up our supplies. Please tell my buddy I love him and miss him at work, and to get well soon and get back here."

John returned home from work, went to the barn and took care of the animals knowing that Mark was sick and would not be able to do his chores. After he had finished, he went to the house to see how his son was doing. Mark stayed in his bed all day because the headache would let up only when he was lying flat. John went into Mark's room and sat on the edge of his bed and told him not to worry since his chores where all done.

After he asked Mark how he was feeling, he told him, "Did you know your friend Joshua got fired? He never showed up for work in a week and a half. Your friend Charlie told me that's what happened. He said you're his buddy and he wants you back with him as soon as you're able to come back to work."

Mark asked where Joshua is now.

"Charlie said he heard he was working at the linseed oil factory but wasn't sure. He also heard that Josh is hanging out at night at some of the local bars. This could get him in trouble. When you are feeling better, even though it's none of my business, I think I will take a ride down and see Fred to find out if I can do anything to help."

Mark stayed home for the rest of the week. It was hard for him to admit that Marlyn and Charlie were dating. He always thought it would be him and Marlyn. The problem was he loved and grew up with Marlyn and her brother Joshua, thinking him and Marlyn would someday marry. Now, it was even harder for him because he and Charlie had become such close friends. He loved Charlie also.

Mary and Tina were preparing to go out teaching in the local area where they lived as instructed by Margaret Fell. Over the past week, she had been in Dennison. She had brought with her some printed leaflets called the 'Watchtower' and 'Awake'. She instructed Mary and Tina to hand them out as they went, even if they came upon a Spanish-speaking family they could not communicate with in English.

Fred had gone out to his fields to check and see if any fence line needed to be repaired and to check on his cattle. Tina took the surrey and went to John and Mary's to help prepare for their teaching weekend. While they were working to put things together, Mary tells Tina about Mark's headaches being back again.

Tina replied to Mary, "Maybe I know what is causing this problem. You know how close Marlyn and Mark have been over the years? Well, did Mark say anything to you about Marlyn having a boyfriend?"

Mary said he had not.

"Well her new boyfriend happens to be Charlie Horan. I understand he and Mark are very close friends. Maybe this is bothering Mark a lot."

Mary answered, "You may be correct. I think I will tell John that I'm going to try to talk to Mark about this, and also get his opinion on whether he thinks this will help."

Tina asked Mary what she thought of Margaret's suggestion that they should attend afternoon classes at the college to learn to speak Spanish.

Mary replied, "No, not me. I don't live in Mexico. Let them learn to speak English if they are going to come or stay in this country!"

Tina replied, "I agree. I tried to talk to Fred about this, and he said the same thing."

Mark stayed in his bedroom all day. The medicine pretty much kept him out of any activity. He therefore heard nothing of the conversation that was held between the ladies and his headache was about gone.

That night, Mary had told John about her conversation with Tina. John was not surprised. He knew that Mark had had strong feelings for Marlyn from the time they were little kids. Mary asked John how he thought they should approach Mark about this.

John replied, "We should talk to him. He needs to understand things cannot and do not always stay the same in our lives."

Mary agreed.

After dinner that evening, they noticed Mark was feeling better, so John said, "Mark, we need to talk."

John went on to explain what Tina had talked to his mom about. Mark acted a little shocked and began to cry.

Mom said, "It's all right, Mark. Don't cry! We do understand how much you thought of her."

"Yes, mom, I love Marlyn and still do. She is dating Charlie and I love him too. He is my best friend ever. It just hurts me, but I will be okay with this; I just need a little time."

John said, "I hope you can come back to work tomorrow. Charlie is asking for you every day."

"Yes, dad. I'm going to go to work and act like nothing has happened."

Charlie had sent a note home to Mark telling him they had a large shipment coming in at the railroad on Friday, and he hoped Mark could make it because he needed the help. Mark went to work on Friday; no way was he going to let his buddy Charlie down when he knew it was not going to be an easy job.

Friday afternoon was payday at the factory. Mr. Horan would walk through the factory and hand out the checks to his employees. Because Mark was such a good worker when he was there, Mr. Horan decided to give him his pay anyway. He gave Mark's check to John because he and Charlie had not returned yet with supplies they were picking up.

"But Mark was not here last week," John told Mr. Horan.

Mr. Horan remarked, "I know, but when Mark is here, he does the work of two men in one week."

John was so proud, he couldn't wait to give the check to Mark and tell him what Mr. Horan had said about him.

Charlie and Mark were too busy checking and loading the supplies they picked up to spend any time talking, except about what was necessary for them to do when they arrived back at the factory, supplies had to be unloaded in areas where they were being used. This could take time.

When finished, Charlie said to Mark, "Thanks, buddy! You sure helped me out so much today. See you Monday."

John had left work at 4:30 p.m. He wasn't going to wait for Mark because he knew they were going to be late getting done, having made three trips to the rail car to pick up all the supplies, and bring them back to the factory. The railroad car had to be empty by morning. John told Mary they had better have a late supper because Mark might not get home until around 7:00 p.m.

Mark arrived home about 7:15 p.m., wiped his horse Diamond down, and put him away. He went in the house and told mom he was very tired, so he would just eat supper and go to bed.

"Dad has something for you, Mark."

John handed Mark his pay check and told him what Mr. Horan had said about him, and how proud he was of him.

Mark ate supper, helped mom with the supper dishes and went to bed.

Mary said to John, "I was cleaning Mark's bedroom today, and in one of the drawers I found some pictures that Mark had drawn of Marlyn and Charlie, and I want to tell you, they look just like them."

"I know, Mary. It's going to take him some time to get over both of them. He loves and respects them so much but says nothing to nobody. I want to tell you, Mr. Horan thinks the world of Mark. I was shocked when he gave him a full pay check and Mark was not there all week."

John asked Mary, "When Tina was here to work with you on your plans to go out teaching, did she say anything to you about Marlyn or Joshua, and what's going on with them?"

"Well, she said that Marlyn was doing well in college all straight A's in her studies. Fred is quite upset with Joshua. He is still working at the linseed oil plant. But he has been running with a wild bunch of guys. He came home last week one night with black eyes. He had been in a fight in one of the local bars. He was damn lucky Officer Reilly wasn't there or he would have been locked up in jail."

"We tried talking to him, but it does no good. He will not even pay attention to us anymore. We wanted him to talk with Margaret Fell while she was here, but he left and went to stay with one of his cronies and never came back home until after she had left. I'm surprised he has even still got his job. You know that he got fired working at Horan's."

"Yes," said John.

"I heard that he and Marlyn used to get along so well, now they don't even talk to each other anymore."

Mary asked Tina about Marlyn's current relationship with Charlie Horan.

Tina replied, "I don't really know. Marlyn doesn't talk much about it. However, she did tell me Charlie was a complete gentleman at all times, and she has the highest amount of respect for him."

Mary asked if Charlie had been to their house.

"Yes, he has," Tina replied. "Mostly on weekends when he's off work, and she is away from college."

"Now I understand why Mark is not interested in coming down here on the weekends anymore. He knows that Charlie might be here, and he doesn't want to get in conversation with him about Marlyn. Mark has been crazy for Marlyn for a long time; now, the problem is he loves Marlyn and Charlie. He always talks about what he and Charlie do together, and it's going to take him some time to get over Marlyn's attraction to Charlie."

"I think that Mark always thought that someday he and Marlyn would marry. It would help him to talk about this situation but he keeps it all to himself and don't want to talk about any of this. I have tried several times to get him to talk to me about Marlyn and Charlie, but he refuses to talk. And when he does, it's always about work and Charlie. He loves Charlie like he was his own brother."

Chapter 10

The two Texas Rangers were down in the Sherman area questioning farmers, farm hands, and neighbors, trying to get a lead on the missing cattle around the city of Sherman's farm land. James Lee Hall, the city Marshall of Sherman, was trying to help the Rangers by questioning some of the farm hands that came into the city on weekends to spend their money. He also was not having much luck trying to get a lead to help with this investigation. Rangers would always travel in pairs just in case they were confronted by a gun happy gunslinger, and there were a few around. Rangers carried the best of weapons. They carried a Colt Peterson five shot revolver, and a 12-gauge side by side scatter gun, also used for hunting.

Spending two weeks in Sherman didn't accomplish much, so the Rangers decided they would go back to Denison and again, question some of the farm laborers. With all the Negros and Mexicans there, somebody had to know something.

Arriving back in Denison, the Rangers stopped at Officer Reilly's office and he advised the Rangers that he had another complaint. Just that morning, two more cattle missing from the same field by Fred Martin. Ranger Bob Chower assured Officer Reilly that they would ride out to the Martin farm to see if they could gather any helpful information. Fred Martin told the Rangers that he went every day to check on the cattle and the day before he had discovered in his count that two more were missing.

"Did you also check the fence line around the field?" asked Ranger Austin.

"Yes, I did each day but found no cut or broken fence, and I checked the gate." replied Fred. "I just could not tell if the fence was cut or pulled apart."

"Okay," replied Austin. "We will take a ride out to the field and check out the gate again."

The two Rangers left and went to the field to inspect the gate entrance. They found that the gate had been pulled apart and re-nailed. They also found wagon wheel tracks on the road near to the entrance to the gate. The Rangers returned to Denison to meet and discuss their findings with Officer Riley. He seemed to know everything that was going on around that town. The first question Ranger Austin asked Reilly was if he had seen any wagons around with heavy wheels made of metal or hard rubber. Reilly hadn't. Ranger Austin told him about the wagon tracks they had found near Fred Martin's cattle field.

Officer Reilly replied, "The only large wagon I have noticed is a wagon that hauls heavy loads from the railroad to its destination. This is a Conestoga wagon built to haul heavy loads and can haul up to 6 tons and is drawn with 4 to 6 horses depending on the load. There is a sign on the side of the wagon that reads 'Rogers Heavy Duty Hauling Near and Far'. I'm sure if you talk to the station master at the railroad, he could tell you whatever they haul for the railroad. Now, if you would like, I can ride up there this afternoon and get you a plaster casting of the wheel tracks."

"Thanks," replied Ranger Austin. "We would appreciate that."

The Rangers decided to wait until the next day to see what would come in on the train as heavy freight. The next morning, the train came into the railroad station, left on its schedule without putting a heavy freight car on the side rail. That was a good time to talk with the station master. However, he could not be of much help to the Rangers. He told them when the heavy loads came in, the papers were already prepared and ready for delivery to the buyer.

Ranger Austin asked, "Who are your primary heavy duty hauler?"

The station master, Mr. Wilson, answered, "We only have one company, and that's Rogers' Heavy Duty Hauling."

"Do you know where they operate out of?"

"No," replied Wilson. "They do have a small place about two miles down the road from here where they keep their horses and wagons. There is no house there. I don't know where they live, but you might try the post office since I would assume they live somewhere in this area."

"Thank you," replied Ranger Austin. "We will do that."

Rangers decided after their discussion that they did not want to make anyone alert to their investigation; so for a while, they would follow that wagon to see where it went. That night, the Rangers decided they would visit a barroom thinking that someone might be talking that could give out a clue on the missing cattle. First, they went to Boland's Saloon. There was a card game going on at a corner table, and five or six men at the bar.

About nine o'clock, a man came in the bar and said, "Boy! There's a fight going on at the Chichet Saloon! Officer Reilly was there to break it up and he arrested some young guy and put him in jail!"

Rangers Crower and Austin left and went over to the Chichet Saloon, and things had quieted down. Everybody from town knew that Reilly was not a person to fool with. He was strong, tough, and very fast with a gun. After Reilly had locked up the kid, he came back to the bar to see that everything was quiet. The saloon keeper offered Reilly a drink for stopping the fight, but he refused the drink. He spotted the Rangers sitting at a table.

"Hi, guys, how are you doing? We just had a little fight here, but it's all taken care of. This is the second time this week this kid has been in trouble. This kid's name is Joshua, and he's the son of Fred and Tina Martin, the family with the missing cattle. I just don't understand that kid. He comes from a nice family; his mother is a special religious teacher along with John Garney's wife. Joshua lost his job at the Horan Factory, went to the linseed oil plant, and just got fired there also for fighting with another employee."

Ranger Austin spoke up and said to Reilly, "It looks like you better keep a close eye on this kid. He could lead you into a bad situation."

"I have that plaster casting of those wagon wheel tracks you requested. They're in my office whenever you want them," says Reilly.

"Thank you," replied Ranger Austin. "We will stop by your office in the morning."

The next day, the Rangers arose early to go down to the rail station to see if the Rogers Heavy Haul wagon was going to show up. They were going to watch from the station, pretending they were waiting for someone coming in on the train. About 8:15 a.m., the train came into the station, but had no heavy side car for delivery. That meant the Rogers wagon would not show up there today. The Rangers then decided to take a ride down the road to the Rogers Hauling barn where the storage barn was located on their property. They wanted to see if they could get a look at the wagons without Rogers knowing about it. When they arrived at the barn, there was no one around. The barn was locked, and it only had one window on the left side. Looking into the window, they saw two wagons; one had large wooden wheels with hard rubber tires mounted on the rims, and the other had small wooden wheels also with hard rubber mounted on the rims.

Both Rangers wondered why the Conestoga wagon had two different sized wheels. They never heard of this before. They suspected they were altered to haul different kinds of freight, but what and how, was the question. The Rangers did not want Rogers to know they were checking on them for any reason and were not ready to stop Rogers on the road and ask questions. They decided to talk to Officer Reilly. Maybe he could secure some information that would help with their suspicions.

The next day the Rangers again went early to the railroad station to see if any heavy freight came in for Rogers to pick up. The train came in with no heavy freight and no side car again. Rogers did not come to the station. About 9:30 a.m., the Rangers rode over to the jailhouse to see Officer Reilly.

"Good morning, Officer Reilly. We came here to see if you could give us any information about the Rogers heavy load operation."

"Gee, I'm sorry. I don't know much about them. I have seen them at the railroad station picking up freight to deliver. When going through the city, they always wave to me as they pass by."

Ranger Austin asked if Reilly had ever stopped them to inspect the wagon.

"No," answered Reilly. "I have had no reason to stop or detain them, and I have never received any complaint against them."

"Can you tell us where their office is located?" asked Austin.

Reilly answered, "I'm sorry, I don't know. It's down in or around Sherman somewhere. I have no idea."

Ranger Bob Chower asked, "Do you think you could help us out by trying to get a little information for us? We don't want them to know that we are looking at them or suspect them of anything."

"Sure," answered Reilly. "Give me a couple of days."

That afternoon Officer Reilly went to see Thomas Horan at the factory. Mr. Horan told Reilly he did buy some heavy equipment sometimes and Rogers Heavy Load Company delivers here to the plant. Other than that, he knew nothing about them. Officer Reilly asked Mr. Horan to please not say anything to anyone that he had been inquiring about them.

Mr. Horan said, "Wait. Let's go talk to my shipping and receiving manager. His name is John Gurney, and he may have an address on them."

John told both of them, "I'm afraid I can't be of much help. When they deliver products here, the invoice shows only their company name as the heading with no address or phone number. I have noticed when they do delivery product, there are two men. They don't talk much at all. They appear to be Mexican and don't speak our language."

Officer Reilly then asked how orders were placed if you needed something.

"We call Pony Express office and they make arrangements to deliver the order. Then, we get confirmation when the order will be delivered or if product is available."

"Thank you, John, for the information. Please say nothing to no one."

The Rangers decided to take the plaster casting that Officer Reilly had managed to get made and to try to match them to the Rogers' wagons.

The next day, they went to the railroad again to see if the train had come in with a heavily loaded side car. It had, and they waited for the Rogers' wagon to come pick up the load. While they were inside the rail car hooking up skid bars to pull the loads from the rail car to the wagon, the Rangers walked from the station where they were, walking quietly up to the wagon and trying to slip the plaster casting over the large wheel on that wagon, but it did not fit. With this, it left the Rangers to believe that the casting might fit the wagon with the small wheels. So not being noticed, they walked away with the casting and then decided they would have to check the other wagon with the small wheels. They decided again to ride down to the barn where the wagon was, knowing it was inside the barn. They had a plan to stake out the barn until the delivery men came back, stay there until dark, and if no one shows, they would be there until the early morning. About 6 p.m., the wagon returned.

Ranger Austin approached it, saw the drivers were Mexican, and said to his partner Captain Chower. "I'll talk to them."

Talking to the two men in Spanish, he told them they were Texas Rangers, and they were there checking wagon wheel sizes for some problems they had. They would also like to see the inside of the wagons. The Mexicans didn't argue and just said okay. Ranger Austin asked them their names.

"I'm Alvero Benito."

"I'm Danato Benito."

The Rangers inspected both wagons. The plaster casting they brought did fit perfectly on the wagon with the small wheels. Ranger Austin asked what the small wheel wagon was used for. Alvero answered for pigs, goats and small horses, but he never said anything about cattle.

Capt. Chower said, "Ask them if they ever hauled cattle with that wagon."

He watched the expressions on their face as Alvero replied, "No, no! Too hard to control the load."

The Rangers said their thank you, and left.

Arriving back in Denison, they went to Officer Reilly's office to discuss this whole matter and to keep Reilly informed and up to date on any information they had. They informed Reilly that the plaster casting that he had taken from the Martin field where the cattle where kept matched the small wheels on the one wagon.

Ranger Austin said, "I questioned both men. They acted very suspicious in the manner they answered the questions. I asked both men where I could find Mr. Rogers and where his office was located. I was very surprised at the answer. They told me that all of the Rogers family perished in the big fire that happened in 1875, that burned down half of the city on the south side of Sherman. They claim that they are running things now. I'm sure there lying, but I have no evidence to be able to arrest them for anything yet. I asked them where they get their delivery orders, and they claimed the pony express drops orders off to them at that location. Again, I believe that's just another big lie. Continuing this investigation, I think tomorrow we will go down to Sherman for a couple days to see if we can find someone that might have known case."

Chapter 11

Mark was having his headache now about every week. He and mom went to see Doctor Bailey and after a preliminary exam, he prescribed an increase in his medication for a couple of weeks to see if it would help. Doctor Bailey asked Mark and his mom if he had any flashbacks with these headaches.

Mark replied, "Yes. I have, mostly about Charlie who I work with. He is my very best friend. I see something heavy falling on him and I can't get to him to help, and I see my dad getting kicked by a horse trying to hook up a wagon for a customer."

Doctor Bailey told them both that when this occurs, he should lie down flat, take his medicine and put an ice pack on the back of his neck. He should not get up until the headache stops. Doctor Bailey asked Mary if Mark had complained about having any problems at work.

"No, he has not. He works with the boss's son, and they are the best of friends. He Loves Charlie; he often says, like a brother."

Mark had never told his mom or dad about Charlie and

Marlyn dating. He didn't think they knew anything about that, but this was one thing on his mind, especially after Charlie talked about her and bragged so much about her.

Working with Charlie the next week was tough on Mark. Charlie asked Mark if he could tell him something about Marlyn.

"I understand your and Marlyn's family were very close and still are today. Both mothers are part time preachers, is that right?"

"Yes," replied Mark. "Joshua and I used to play together as kids. I can't tell you much about Marlyn because she spent her time with her mother. I never heard anything bad about Marlyn, but I guess her brother Joshua had started getting into trouble. You know he lost his job at the factory and linseed oil plant. I heard he's been getting in fights and has been hanging out in some of the bars in town. His mom and dad have tried talking to him, but he will not listen."

"Well, Mark, I have to tell you because you are my buddy. I have been seeing Marlyn on weekends lately. I have been to her house and met her parents. They were very nice to me. Marlyn is doing a good job in college and she is on the honor roll again, and also on the Dean's list this semester. She works and studies hard. I'm doing okay but not setting the world on fire. Accounting classes are not easy."

Mark went home that night feeling pretty down over Marlyn. So, he decided to talk to mom after supper. After eating, John went out to the barn to brush down his horse Jenny and Mark's horse Diamond. That was a good time to talk to mom while they were doing dishes.

"Mom, I have a question for you. Did I do something wrong?" He told her about Marlyn and Charlie's relationship and asked, "What did I do wrong? I always thought it would be me and Marlyn!"

Mom replied, "No, you have done nothing wrong. This happens to people when they fall in love. I have known about this for weeks from Tina but didn't want to upset you. Someday, the right girl will come along, and the same thing could happen to you."

"I would not feel so bad, but it's my best friend Charlie she has fallen for! Now I know why she has been so distant to me lately. I wonder how her brother Joshua feels about this."

Mom answered, "I don't think it makes much difference with him. He's never home and is going down the wrong path, getting in fights and hanging out in some of the bars in town. He's already been twice in jail."

"Thanks, mom, for the talk. I will try harder to better understand. It just hurts when Charlie talks about her all the time while I'm working with him."

Monday morning, it's off to work. John left for work at 6:30 that morning, and Mark left at 7:15 a.m. It was a nice sunny day with low humidity. Everything seemed to appear like a normal work day. No, it didn't work out that way. That afternoon, Charlie and Mark went to the railroad station to pick the order for the plant. Charlie was talking about Marlyn all the way to the station, as they were unloading the rail car, a large box fell off the top of the pile knocking Charlie down and pinning him against the side wall. Mark tried to remove the box, but it was too heavy for him alone. Charlie was hurting.

Mark yelled out the door to a railroad yard man, and he helped Mark get the box off Charlie, who appeared to be having trouble breathing. Mark drove him down to the hospital, and Charlie was checked out by a doctor. He was okay and no broken bones. So, they picked up their load and proceeded to the plant.

When they arrived, the receiving man said, "Hey, guys, there has been an accident here. John got kicked by a horse while he was trying to hook up the team to a new wagon. They took him down to the hospital. Think he may have a broken leg."

This happened just as Mark's flashback told him.

Charlie told Mark to go down to the hospital to see how his dad was doing. "Don't worry about me. I'll get another worker out of the plant to help unload the supplies."

Mark hurried to the hospital to see his dad. When he arrived, the emergency room nurse told Mark to go in and see the doctor. Doctor A.L. Jones talked to Mark and told him he had given his dad a sedative for pain and had examined him the best he could (there were no x-ray machines invented yet).

"I believe the large bone may be cracked but not broken. There was some swelling in the leg, but I could not feel any sign of a broken leg. Very possible it's a bone fracture. I have prepared a splint for his leg. He is to stay off his feet for five to six weeks, and he cannot ride his horse. I want to see him either here or in my office before he goes back to work." Doctor Jones told Mark he could go home but it must be on the back of a wagon as his dad was not to try to mount a horse or even try to sit in a surrey.

Mark told his dad, "I'm going to go get Fred to come with his wagon to help get you home. Maybe I can have Tina go tell mom about the accident while we are here to pick you up."

Mark rode to Fred and Tina's house, told them about the accident at the plant with dad. Tina agreed she would take the surrey, and go to see Mary and tell her John is on his way home from the hospital. Fred hitched up the wagon and put some heavy quilts and blankets on the back. He and Mark went to the hospital to pick up John and take him home.

Arriving at the hospital, Doctor Jones gave those instructions on how to handle John when they got him home. Two of the hospital team helped Fred and Mark carry John out on a stretcher, place him gently in the back of the wagon. From St. Luke's Hospital, it was about three and a half miles to John's home. This was a rough ride for John on the back of a hay wagon and by the time they got him home he was having quite a bit of pain. They had to wait an hour for the pain to let up so they could carry him in the house to his bed. Fred and Tina was on front of the stretcher and Mark and his mom on the back. They managed to slide him off the back of the wagon and get him in his bed. In less than five minutes, he fell asleep.

Mary remarked to Fred and Tina, "I can't thank you guys enough for being there for me. I don't know what I would do without you!"

Fred replied, "We have been close friends for many years, like family. We will always be there for you."

John had a restless night, waking up in pain when he moved. Mary didn't sleep well either, trying to help John as much as she could.

Mark awoke at 6:00 a.m., and was going to go into work early thinking he would work in dad's place to help keep things going well. When he arrived at work, Mr. Horan had already placed another man in doing John's job. Mark was a little confused, so he asked Mr. Horan why he was not put on his dad's job. Mr. Horan replied to Mark telling him that the man he had placed on that job had been with the company for a long time and has plenty of experience knowing that job. "Besides, Mark, I really need you in the shipping and receiving department. You have done a great job at that post. My son, Charlie, brags about you all the time, telling me what a good job you do and how well organized you are. I think that Charlie would have a fit if I even suggested placing you in another position. Don't worry, you will be getting a raise in pay starting the end of this month. You will be making as much money as your dad was at his job. I will be coming to your house this weekend to see your dad, to bring him his paycheck and see how he's doing."

Mark was so excited about going home to tell his dad what Mr. Horan said about how he was going to get a raise in pay at the end of the month. He was very happy being told that he was doing a great job and Mr. Horan wanted him to stay in the shipping and receiving department. However, that afternoon did not turn out to be such a great afternoon for Mark.

Charlie came to his department after lunch time. He said to Mark, "We need to go down to the train. There are some supplies there waiting for us, and they were heavy stuff, so I will need your help."

Mark answered, "No problem; I'll be right with you."

Everything was going fine until they started going for the pickup at the train station. Charlie speaks up and says to Mark, "Hey! I have a surprise to tell you about. Marlyn and I are now engaged, and plan to get married right after our college graduation. I would like you to be my best man at the wedding!"

Mark agreed, only because of his love for Charlie. But his heart was hurting because he really felt love for Marlyn. Mark was now feeling his hurt, thinking if he had graduated from high school and gone to college, that Marlyn might have paid attention more to him. He knew there was nothing he could do about it now, and would just have to accept things just the way they were. He was also somewhat disappointed that Marlyn did not come and tell his family about her engagement.

Everything appeared to be sliding downhill for Mark in the way he felt. He's starting to get his headaches back a couple times a week and once in a while flashbacks, very quick and not lasting long. Mark had made an appointment for the next day to see Doctor Bailey. He wanted to see if he could increase his medicine amount.

That next morning, Doctor Bailey again gave Mark a preliminary examination and questioned him concerning his activities and his job stress. Mark informed him that were no problems on his job and none at home either.

Doctor Bailey asked, "Do you black out when you get these attacks?"

Mark answered, "No, but heavy pain when it first starts,

then it lets up in a few minutes after I take the medicine."

Doctor Bailey told Mark, "I am going to increase your medication a little. I want you to continue taking the same as I have prescribed. See me next Friday at 2:00 p.m. Tell your dad I will be up past your place tomorrow and will stop by to see him. Doctor Jones at the hospital told me about your dad's broken or fractured leg. He feels badly that he could not have enough time to get away from the hospital, but asked me to stop and see your dad and take a look at his leg to see how it's doing."

Mark thanked the doctor and said he would tell dad when he got home. Mark and Diamond headed for home. On the way again, two Mexican men riding down towards Denison looked at Mark and said nothing but both were laughing hard as they passed him. Still a little confused, Mark paid no attention to them, thinking they had been drinking anyway. They looked like they were half drunk and could hardly sit up straight in their saddles.

Upon arriving home, Mark tied Diamond to the post, entered the house, and said hello to his mother. "I have a message for dad. Doctor Bailey is going to stop here tomorrow to see him and take a look at his leg, as requested by Doctor Jones."

"Good!" replied John, "Then maybe I can find a way to get out of this bed!"

Mark said, "Great, but you're not going anywhere anyway. I'm going out to take care of the horses and feed the animals. I forgot to tell you dad, I saw the Mexican guys on the way home. They were still laughing at me but said nothing. They look like they had been drinking."

Dad replied, "Just pay no attention to them, and keep on riding."

Just as Mark finished his chores and started towards the house, he saw the Martin's coming up the road. He had no idea that his mom had invited them for supper that night. Fred was riding his horse alongside the surrey with Tina and Marlyn. Mark wondered why Marlyn had come with them.

Mary was preparing the supper while they all went into the bedroom to visit with John. Mark was feeling a little uncomfortable sitting beside Marlyn while visiting with dad.

Mary addressed Mark and said, "Would you please lead our guests into dinner prayer while I go sit with your dad for our prayers?"

Mark felt a little bashful but he did as mom had asked. After supper, Mark got up and started to pick up dishes.

Mary said, "No, Mark, Tina and I will do dishes. Why don't you and Marlyn go sit on the front porch and visit?"

Marlyn and Mark went to the front porch and sat down to talk. "I heard you and Charlie are engaged to marry. Why didn't you tell me?"

"Because Charlie wanted to tell you himself. He so badly wants you to be his best man and witness. Charlie loves you like a brother; he talks about you all the time."

"Why did you agree to marry Charlie?"

"Because I love him so much."

That answer hurt Mark, so he said no more. Marlyn

could see what was happening, so she got up and went in the house. Marlyn told her mother that she was ready to go home whenever she was. She was a little disgusted with Mark and the way he acted. She knew that Mark always liked her while she liked him as a friend. She never told him she loved him or wanted to be his girlfriend. Mary and Tina knew pretty much what was going on and this was a good time to bring it out in the open.

Mary said, "I talked with Mark once, but not in any detail. I will have another talk with him to try to make him understand that life does not always go our way. Each one of us has the right to choose our own life."

Fred came out of the bedroom. He knew nothing about what was going on. Fred told Tina and Marlyn to go say goodbye to John, then they'd better head for home before it starts getting dark. Fred asked where Mark was.

Mary replied, "Oh, I guess he went back out to the barn. He claimed he had something he had to do before dark."

"Okay, tell Mark we said goodnight. We'd better get going."

Mark stood inside the barn door looking out, crying and watching them leave. Before he went back to the house, he tried so hard to hide his true love for Marlyn and did not want to let it out to anyone.

John asked where Mark was.

"Oh, he just forgot to do something in the barn. He went back to get it done before dark. He will be in shortly."

Chapter 12

The Texas Rangers had been gone for a while trying to get information that would lead them to the bandits who were steeling beef cattle all over north Texas. On information they had secured while traveling, they returned to Denison to meet with Officer Reilley to discuss leads they had secured, in hopes they could soon make an arrest. The year was now currently 1899.

Ranger Bob Chower and Stephan Austin went to Officer Reilley's office in Denison. Ranger Chower asked him if he had any further information or complaints concerning theft of cattle while they were gone from the area. Officer Reilly hadn't received any complaints of losses in the past few months.

Ranger Chower said to Reilly, "We have our suspicions with a couple of good leads, but we need proof before we can make an arrest."

Officer Reilly asked how he could help.

Ranger Chower replied, "You know, now most of the people here know we are Rangers. This makes it difficult for us to do surveillance where we need to. We would like you to check the local bars here at night to see if

134

you can pick up any information on these two people: Alvero Benito and his brother Danato Benito."

Officer Reilly replied to the Rangers, "I'm in good with some of the bartenders at the local bars and I will check them out to see if I can get any information for you."

"Something else I would like to tell you. We checked on the Rogers family down in Sherman and what we found was indescribable. On May 15, 1886, a tornado came through the south Sherman area destroying some fifty homes, killing between fifty to eighty people. The Rogers family were burned up in the fire that occurred. We checked with the City Clerk, and there was no business filing under the Rogers name. We did talk to some people in south Sherman, and we met a lady who knew the Rogers family. She told us they were a nice family that seemed to have everything they wanted, but never said anything about running any business. We were unable to find out now who owns the Rogers Heavy Hauling business. When we questioned the two Mexicans about that, they claimed Mr. Rogers gave the business to them before he died. We don't believe that because he perished in the fire with his whole family," Ranger Austin said to Reilly. "We suspect these two Mexicans somehow are involved with the cattle theft, not only here but all over north Texas. We must obtain information on this before we can take action. We will be staying at the Denison hotel, and you can contact us there if needed. City Marshal James Lee Hall will be checking the bars in Sherman for us in hopes he may get more information on the Rogers family, like how long did they live in Sherman, where did they come here from, did they own the Rogers Heavy Hauling Business, as such."

Officer Reilly answered, "Okay, Rangers, I will be in touch should I be lucky to secure some helpful information for you."

The Rangers decided they would stay away from all the local bars to give the Officers a chance to obtain information for them. Instead, they decided they would go on a night stakeout near the barn where the wagons were being kept. It was a nice moonlit night. The Rangers decided to hide in the wooded area across from the barn since there was no field there and heavy brush cover that side of the road. It would be hard for anybody to see them there even with the bright moon that night.

About 3:30 in the morning, they heard a wagon coming up the road. They could see that there were four horses pulling the wagon and it was the one with the small wheels. The barn was long and large with large double doors on both ends. As they approached the barn, they drove around the back of the barn and entered, while one man opened the large doors on both ends. There were four horses drawing this wagon. The Rangers decided to stay out of sight and watch what happened next. They had pulled the wagon into the barn about halfway to the center of the barn. The wagon with the large wheels sat to the right side of where they had parked this wagon. Having only lanterns and flashlights, it was difficult to see everything going on inside the barn. The four horses where unhitched from the wagon and placed in a large penned in area on the left side of the wagons. The two men got large pails of water and were washing the inside of the wagon.

Ranger Austin said to his partner, "I would love to know what they are trying to wash out of that wagon!"

About a half hour later, the two men brought their two Appaloosa riding horses out of the barn, saddled and ready to go. They padlocked both end doors and left. The Rangers decided it would do no good trying to get inside the barn trying to gather evidence and decided to follow the men. The Rangers followed them down the road towards Sherman, staying about a quarter of a mile behind them because of the bright moon light. About five miles south of Sherman, they turned on a dirt road to the left, went about a half mile, then up to a house that looked empty and appeared to be half falling down. They rode behind the house to an old small barn, put the horses inside and walked back around to the front of the house and entered from the front. The back of the house looked like it had been falling down.

Ranger Austin said to Ranger Chower, "Let's go back and get some rest. The next time they go out on a heavy load haul, we can follow or come back here to the house to see what we can find."

Ranger Chower agreed saying, "Good idea. I think if we come back here to the house, it will not take much to get into the house to see what we can find. It appears no one else is living there. Maybe we can get in and out without them even knowing we were there."

Officer Reilly had been checking the local bars in the Denison City area, but so far no signs of them showing up, no discussion about heavy hauling yet. On the way back, they stopped at Marshal James Lee Hall's office, and he said the same thing. So far he had not also seen or heard anything about these guys.

The Rangers arrived back in Denison and went directly

to the Eclipse livery stable where they kept their horses while they were in town. Big John, the blacksmith and part owner of the stable, was friendly with the Rangers. While cleaning and preparing the stable for their horses, Big John got in conversation with the Rangers, not knowing who they were looking for or why.

Big John said, "Boy! I was busy last week. I had two of Rogers' heavy hauling horses in here to have new shoes put on. This reminded me of what I thought was strange. About a week ago, I was down to Sherman to get some things I needed. On my way back to Denison, I passed Rogers Heavy Hauling wagon and the two men waved to me as we passed each other. The strange thing about it was that I could have sworn I heard cattle mooing as we passed."

Ranger Austin said, "That's not so strange. What kind of wagon did they have? One with big wheels or small wheels?"

Big John replied, "It had small wheels and was covered with a large canvas."

"Any idea where they were headed?"

"No." replied John. "They may have been headed to Fort Worth. There is a large meat packing plant there."

Ranger Chower asked Big John not to say anything or discuss this with anyone. Big John knew the Rangers were looking for cattle rustlers in north Texas.

John replied, "Don't worry. I will say nothing to anyone about our conversation."

"Thank you. We are working hard to try to make an arrest on this case. We appreciate your cooperation."

The Rangers wanted so badly to arrest Alvero and Danato Benito of the Rogers Heavy Hauling Equipment Company. But first, they needed to have proof they were hauling stolen cattle on one of the wagons. Also, they needed to find out if there were others involved in this crime of stolen cattle. Ranger Chower sent a message to the Ranger's main office explaining so far what they have found in their investigation, and requesting a couple of Rangers to assist in the investigation in and around the Fort Worth area, suggesting they go in as undercover agents trying to get a job in the slaughterhouse and the large meat packing plant. The letter was brought to Homer Garrison Jr., Director of the Texas Rangers. He examined the report and agreed with Ranger Chower and sent a reply back saying that the Ranger office approved, and would send a couple of their best investigators within a week to Fort Worth. Will keep you advised.

William B. Travis was in charge of the Texas Rangers' arrest and proof of all information supplied by the investigators. If necessary to obtain a warrant for an arrest, Cornell Travis also contacted the judge covering the County where the arrest was being made to obtain the warrants. Texas Rangers became very well known in the State, and respected for their devotion to duty, and at times, they had to use their guns to protect themselves when trying to arrest someone for a crime they had committed.

Investigating Rangers were well trained in how to obtain information when trying to make arrest. In the years of 1894 and 1895, the Rangers scouted 173,391 miles, made 676 arrests and returned 2,855 head of stolen livestock to their owners. In the year of 1895, Alvero and Danato Benito were arrested and the Rogers Heavy Hauling was confiscated and put out of business.

Fred Martin did not get his beef cattle back, instead he was paid with money secured while making the arrest and proving that the cattle stolen from the Martin farm did in fact belong to him.

Chapter 13

Mark was a very devoted and loving type guy, especially to his family and friends. He was also a good worker at no matter what job he was assigned to do. Mr. Horan liked Mark, like he was also his son. He worked hard and saved his money, spending only what was necessary for the things he or his family needed.

Charlie Horan was Mark's very best friend. They acted like brothers when they were together– laughing, joking, playing games on each other, and working together most of the time in the shipping department. Mark could see the changes coming more and more. Lately, Charlie was asked to work in the office with his dad. Mark understood because Charlie was in college and doing very well in his business administration courses. It took a while for Mark to understand Charlie and Marlyn being together, thinking it was because they were both college students.

Mark's parents did a lot to help him understand everything. Now, he was getting himself prepared to be the best man at their wedding like Charlie had asked him to be. Plans were being made for the wedding of Marlyn and

Charlie. They had agreed that the wedding would be held at the Horan home and ranch. Mark's mother, Mary Gurney, would perform the wedding ceremony out of the book of Mormons Bible.

At 1:00 p.m. on June 10th, 1899. The reception would also be held at the Horan ranch after the wedding, the invited guest would be welcomed and a fine dinner would be presented. Gifts would be presented to the bride and groom, followed by dancing with the college band. This would be a formal wedding, the ladies and bridesmaids would be wearing pretty long gowns, and the men will be dressed also in tuxedos. Marlyn had chosen a very light soft blue for her wedding dress. Charlie wanted his men to wear black, either in suits or tuxes. Since it might be a hot day at that time of year, the wedding would be held in the large entertainment room that was built off the side of the main house to provide an area for business meetings and out of town business people.

Mr. Horan asked Charlie, "Have you talked to your college buddies about no excessive drink at this wedding? It will not be allowed."

Charlie did assure his dad it will not happen. "They have promised me, and I believe them."

This was about three months before the wedding. The date was March 12, 1898. Mark went to Hayes' Gentlemen's Clothing Store in Denison to purchase his tux for the wedding. Mr. Hayes tried to convince Mark to rent the tux because it was cheaper than buying. Mark believed if you're paying money to buy the tux then you own it, so he paid cash and purchased the tux. Mark was doing pretty well with his adjustment to his friend Marlyn getting married to his buddy Charlie. He loved both of them so much. Mark was taught as a baby by his mom and dad, and the family bible that you must love and respect all others regardless of who they are or maybe. Jehovah has given us all our right to make choices.

The next day, while they were working, Charlie says to Mark, "Hey! Got to tell you this. After Marlyn finishes college, dad is going to offer her a job in the office, at least part time until she gets her job to intern at the hospital. Don't you think that's great?"

Mark replied, "Yes, your dad is a kind and a great guy." Mark didn't feel as great about that as he would get to see Marlyn everyday.

Everything seemed to be going well at both the Martin and Gurney family homes. Mr. Martin had gotten paid for his missing cattle, thanks to the Texas Rangers. The Martin's daughter, Marlyn, was getting married soon, and Joshua had gotten himself straightened out and had gone for training to become a Texas Ranger. The Gurney family, Mark has been doing well had had no bad headaches and no strange flashbacks lately. Dad John had recovered well from his broken leg and was back to work now. Tina Martin and Mary Gurney were working hard on their teaching of the Mormon and Holy Bible to all that would listen.

Every Sunday morning, they would meet and travel to a distance in a day of about five miles below Sherman and all around villages outside the city of Denison. The village people were very happy to see them come every week and give them a chance to learn about God. Little did any of them know that a tragic event was about to happen to one of the families that would change the lives of both families forever.

Charlie and Marlyn where busy trying to make the final arrangements for their upcoming wedding. Mark had finally accepted the love for both Charlie and Marlyn, his two best friends, and was very happy being part of the wedding as best man. Mark's mom, Mary, being an active Mormon teacher, had taught Mark that love for all people was so important in his life. Learn to love yourself with others and you will have a happy life. Mark was a good young man, saying his prayers everyday for his friends and families who he knew. He had a heart full of love until disaster struck, and that would change his life.

It was now June 3rd, the week before the wedding in 1897. Mark had just had a birthday and was now 24 years old. It was a nice beautiful day, sun shining and no rain. After breakfast, Mark was helping mom with the dishes and dad went out to the barn to do some repair work he had started.

Mark said, "Mom, I'm going out to the barn to feed the animals and see if I can help dad with anything."

Mom said, "Okay, Mark. I have some studying to do today, so I need some peace and quiet."

John had put up a ladder to nail in some boards on the upper part of the barn. The boards were parallel, spaced about 1 inch apart to allow the air to blow into the upper part of the barn to help keep the barn cool. John finished his job and said, "Mark, I'm going into the house now to visit with Mom."

Mark replied, "Okay."

Mark was still in the barn feeding and watering the horses and the rest of the animals. He's also doing some cleaning up. It was about 2:45 in the afternoon when Mark had climbed up the inside ladder to arrange some food storage for the animals. While moving some baskets around, he thought he heard his dad saying a loud "No!" to somebody. Mark ran to the wall to look out and saw three men who appeared to be Mexican as they were all wearing sombreros. Two of the men shot and killed his dad standing on the porch. Mom came running out to the porch when the other man pulled his gun and shot her. All three appeared to be drunk. As they rode out of the yard past the barn, Mark got a good look at all three faces. Mark stumbled down the ladder and went running to the house. Dad John was dead, shot through the forehead. Mom Mary was still alive, but was shot in the chest and slowly dying. She tried to whisper something to Mark and he thought she said to get them, but actually said hide from them. Mark was in total shock and could not even cry. He picked them up, carried them into the house and laid them on the floor, side by side. He ran to the barn and grabbed his horse Diamond and a saddle and, went flying to the Martin's home.

Fred and Tina where both home. Marlyn was at college.

Fred told Mark, "You stay there and I would go get Officer Reilly and be right back."

Fred grabbed Diamond and went as fast as he could to Denison to get Officer Reilly. He told Reilly what had happened.

"Where is Mark now?" sked Reilly.

"He is at my house. My wife is with him. He is in total shock."

Reilly said, "I must go talk to him now. I will inform every law enforcement agency in the state by teletype."

Arriving back at Fred's house, Officer Reilly asked Mark if he could tell him how this had happened. Mark proceeded to tell him what he had seen but he did not tell Reilly he could identify their faces. Mark seem to have a photographic memory, like taking a picture. He also was a very good artist and could draw a face on a piece of paper and it would look exactly like that person.

Mark agreed and allowed Officer Reilly to notify the undertaker in Denison to pick up the bodies and prepare the bodies for the burial. Fred and Tina bought a 4-person lot in Fairview cemetery for the Gurney family. Fred and Tina wanted Mark to stay at their house for a while. Mark thanked them but said he had animals and needed to be home for them. Fred understood and said for Mark to let him know if he needed help. Fred thought maybe it would be good for Mark to be home alone. It might help him to recover some.

Mark said, "Thank you for supper. I must go home now to take care of the animals. Thank you for your help."

Before Mark arrived back home, the undertaker had been there and picked up the bodies. Mark entered the house, walked over to Mom and Dad's bedroom door and closed it, never to enter it again. He went to his bedroom, grabbed three sheets of poster paper and his pens. He sat down at the kitchen table and drew pictures of all three of the men that looked exactly like them.

Marlyn had come home from her day at college not knowing what had happened to Mark's family. When Fred and Tina had explained it to her, she broke down sobbing.

After a little while, she said to Mom, "I must go tell Charlie now!"

Fred said, "No, daughter. I think you'd better let me go. I must tell Charlie's family what has happened. Don't forget, it was Charlie's dad, Thomas E. Horan, who hired both Mark and John."

"Okay. Thanks dad. Glad I don't have to go."

Both mom and I are so upset that we can't stop crying.

Mark did manage to get to the barn to take care of the animals, but when he returned to the house, suddenly, he developed a bad headache and all he could see was the three Mexicans that killed his parents. He grabbed his medicine and laid down on his bed just to rest; no way could he sleep. Mark was having a lot of pain, so he doubled his prescribed dose. About a half hour later, the pain stopped, and the medicine knocked him out cold. Mark had changed a lot in his mind. He failed to say his prayers like taught by his mom, and he still had not shed a tear for his mom and dad.

The Funeral arrangements were being made by their friends, Fred and Tina Martin. They had purchased a lot for the two families at the Fairview Cemetery in Denison, because they wanted to be near the Gurney family when they died. Fred was not going to let Mark pay for any of it. Fred, Tina, Joshua, and Marlyn were also having a tough time with the murder of their best friends. For years, they were like the rest of the family to them.

That next morning, Fred said to Tina, "I think I better take a ride to the Gurney home to see how Mark is doing."

Tina replied, "Yes, please go. I just cannot go to that house for now. Tell Mark we are praying for him and the family every day and night."

"Okay, I will be gone all day, so don't worry. Going to check our cattle in the field to see if they're okay. Want to be sure there is no fence broken anywhere."

That afternoon, Charlie had ridden up to the house to see Marlyn, knowing it was going to be tough on her. The Gurney family was part of her life also. Charlie and Marlyn were crying together for a long time out of their strong love for Mark and his family.

After Charlie was able to calm Marlyn down, he said to Marlyn, "Honey, you realize it is too late to postpone our wedding. We have over one hundred people coming with all the business associates with my dad. I don't know what to tell Mark. He was to be my best man, and I know he is not going to want to come to a wedding when his parents have not even had their funeral yet. Please let me explain this to you to see how you feel about it. I have a college friend who knows what has happened and he is willing to stand up for me if Mark cannot come. His name is Frank Bannor, a real nice guy. I'm sure you would like him. So, what do you think about this?"

Marlyn replied, "It sounds all right to me, Charlie. Do what you have to."

"Well, I'm sorry, my love, because I have already invited

him and he has agreed to do it for me." This was a difficult time for everyone. The funeral for the Gurney's was to be held the day after the wedding.

Mark was at home still drawing pictures of the three men that killed his parents. He then said a prayer for both mom and dad. That was the last prayer he would say for anyone. As the day moved on, Mark became more bitter in his mind and could not understand how God could let this happen to them.

That afternoon, Mr. Martin showed up to talk to Mark about his plan to live, and where. Also, about the wedding and the funeral.

Fred said to Mark, "Why don't you let me take the three horses down to my barn? I would be glad to help you care for them. You can bring Diamond down to see them anytime."

Mark replied to Fred, "You're right. I appreciate your help. Let's take them down this afternoon."

They walked over to the barn and got the horses ready to move down to Fred's barn. Mark took dad's horse, and Fred took mom's two horses.

Marlyn had gone to her bedroom when she saw Mark and her dad come in the yard with the horses. She did not want to even try to talk to Mark out of love and respect for him. Fred asked Mark very nicely what his plans for the wedding and the funeral were.

Mark replied to Fred, "I'm not going to the wedding, not even sure I will attend the funeral. Don't know how I will feel." Mark had a few mixed emotions about his future. He wondered about his job, his headaches and medication, and his anger in an effort to track down the three men that he will be trying to find. He already had in mind what he was going to do, and it did not involve turning them in to the police.

Mark decided that he would go see Doctor Bailey next week as he was getting low on his medicine. Mr. Horan had talked to Mark after what had happened, and told him not to worry about his job, and gave him a month's salary to give him time to recover from the terrible event. Mark had decided he would take a couple of weeks off to see how he could adjust to this situation. He was a very loyal and faithful employee who worked hard at his job every day. He did well at saving his money earned each week.

The next day was the wedding. Mark did not attend. He felt bad, but just not able to handle it right now. He decided to save the clothes for the next day for the funeral. Yes, he knew he would go to see his parents for the last time. The wedding went off well. Frank Bannor did show up as best man for Charlie. Fred walked his daughter down the aisle for her marriage. The reception went well with about ninety-five people showing up. Mark was at home trying not to think about the wedding he missed because he loved them both.

A big surprise happened at the wedding. Just as the wedding began, in walked Marlyn's brother Joshua. The family had not seen him for months after he left home. All were surprised when they saw him, not knowing that he had straightened himself out and had now became a graduated Texas Ranger. When his Mom and Marlyn saw him, they started to cry. After dad had walked Marlyn down the aisle, he turned around and walked back to where

Joshua was sitting, sat down beside him, and kissed him on the cheek, being so proud that Joshua had come home not even knowing that his sister was getting married.

The reception started at once. After the first dance by the husband and wife, Marlyn ran over and grabbed her brother while still crying, and got him on the dance floor. She's so happy and proud of her brother, Texas Ranger Joshua who had come home just in time for her wedding. What the family didn't know was that the Texas Ranger office in Waco, Texas had received the message by teletype that a double murder had happened in Denison.

The Training Commander called Joshua into his office and told Joshua, he was going to send him to Denison because he lived there and would be familiar with that area, and he may get information that could lead to the killers.

Chapter 14

The next morning, the day of the funeral, Mark suddenly awoke with a slight headache. As he got out of bed, the headache developed stronger and stronger. He took his medicine and laid down. All he could see in his mind was the three men that had killed his parents. About an hour later, the headache let up. He knew just what he was going to do after the funeral – visit the nearest gun shop.

Since Mark was not able to attend the wedding, he did not know that Joshua was in town or that he was a Texas Ranger. Suddenly, there was a knock at the door. Mark looked out to see Joshua standing there.

Mark opened the door and said, "Hey Joshua! How are you doing? It's so good to see you, my old buddy!"

Joshua replied, "Mark, I am here on business. You know that I am now a Texas Ranger, and I heard about the murder of your parents. I am going to the funeral today with you. I have known that you have special powers by the visions you can see in your mind since we were kids together, so I do need you to help me catch these killers. Can you tell me how this all happened? Maybe after the funeral."

Mark replied, "I just can't talk about it now."

Joshua said that it wasn't a problem and they would talk later. They talked for a while, then rode down to Denison to attend the funeral at 1 pm that afternoon. It was quite a surprise that there where over one hundred people attending. Mr. Horan had closed his factory for that day in respect for both Mark and his dad who both worked there. Tina, Mary's best girlfriend had a rough time doing the sermon, trying hard not to cry while preaching. Charlie and Marlyn were both in tears during the whole service. Mark stood there by the caskets and never shed a tear. Everybody that was there and knew Mark knew that he was in deep shock. Texas Ranger Joshua was standing beside Mark to help him if needed, with tears streaming down, also.

After the service, people came up to express their condolences and give Mark a hug. Fred asked Mark to come over to the house for evening dinner that night, but Mark refused, saying thank you, and that he wanted to get home.

Fred replied, "I understand you want to be alone. Joshua and I will be up to see you in the morning."

Mark really wanted to get rid of Joshua for the rest of that day, so he could go to the gun Shops in Denison to buy a gun that he would say was for his own protection, in case the Mexicans came after him. But no. He wanted to practice, then go after them.

Tina said to Fred, "Did you notice that Mark never shed a tear during the funeral and not even when he bent over to kiss his mom in the casket?"

"Yes, I did," replied Fred. "Everyone was crying then.

But I noticed a very hard look on Mark's face. I am very worried about him. I sure hope he does not do anything stupid, like going to buy a gun to shoot himself to be with his parents. I know he has to be crying on the inside."

Joshua was also quite concerned about Mark and wanted to stay with him when he went home, but Mark insisted he go with his parents because he wanted some alone time. Joshua didn't want to upset Mark and he love Mark like his brother.

Joshua said to Mark, "Okay, I will see you in the morning and we will talk about things. I will find these guys and they will get their justice."

Mark never answered Joshua. He just wanted to get him out of sight, so he could get to a gun shop somewhere in that area. Joshua rode with Mark out of town until the road split. That's where they split; Joshua toward his home, and Mark to his home. Mark waited until Joshua got out of sight, then rode back into town. He rode back into Denison to look for a gun shop.

He found the F & I Pawn Shop. They were the biggest gun shop in the area. Mark knew nothing about guns, not even how to load one. He talked to the store manager, Mr. Franklin, and explained that he needed advice because he or his family had never owned a gun. The Manager asked Mark if he was going to use it to go hunting. He replied said he wanted the gun for personal protection. Mr. Franklin took him over to the pistol case to look at the guns, and Mark asked him what he would recommend. The manager replied all his guns were good and Mark should pick the one he liked. He looked into the case and saw a Colt Peterson 5-shot revolver, built in 1837

& 1838. He held the gun in his hand and it seem to fit his hand just right to hold. Mark bought the gun, a gun belt, and box of ammo. Mr. Franklin told Mark he needed to hold this gun firmly in his hand as he shoots, because it does have quite a kick when fired. Mark bought the gun and a good leather holster and a box of bullets also a reload casing kit.

The next morning, Joshua, the Texas Ranger, rode up to Mark's house to see if he was okay and to have a talk with Mark. Mark showed the gun to Joshua and what he had bought at the gun shop. Joshua asked Mark what he intended to do with this gun.

Mark replied, "I just need it for protection in case those guys discover that I was there at the time and decide to come after me."

"That's okay, but I want to explain something to you to try to understand. As a Texas Ranger, it is my job to track these guys down and arrest them for murder and prosecute them to the full extent of the law. Don't worry. They will stand trial and pay the price."

Mark listened to what he had to say but never answered, thinking to himself *I will find them hopefully before you and they will all be dead.* Joshua knew damn well that Mark never listened to him. Joshua asked Mark if he still drew pictures of what he saw. Mark replied that he'd lost his touch and didn't draw at all anymore. Joshua knew Mark was lying because he was an excellent natural artist. Mark did not want to give him realistic pictures of these men because in his mind, he wanted to track them down and kill them first.

Joshua said to Mark, "We have been like brothers

since we were kids. Please, Mark! Think before you act. Don't get the idea that you want to go after these guys. They are murderers, and if you find and kill them, you also will be a murderer. I sure as hell don't want to have to arrest you for murder."

Mark replied, "Yes. Don't worry. I'm only going to do what's right. You know I have a right to protect myself." Mark could hardly wait until Josh left.

That afternoon when it was quite, Mark sat on the porch practicing to load and reload his pistol with the safety on. He put his gun down, and went to load two old sand buckets and put them on the trunk of a couple of tree trunks, so he could have something to shoot at for practicing. He then loaded his gun belt with bullets and went out back of the house to practice. He shot his first five shots and never once hit one of the sand pails. He reloaded his gun and shot again, and still didn't hit the sand buckets, so he moved closer to the buckets and shot all five shots again. This time he was about 25 feet away and hit the target with three of his shots. Mark was eager to learn how to shoot but thought he could learn to do it all by himself. So, he quit for the day and decided he would practice every day for at least one hour. He knew it would take a while to become good with a gun.

A week had gone by and Mark had practiced shooting for an hour every day. He had improved a little but still not enough to be good with his gun. One afternoon, that week while he was practicing, a man came riding up the road and heard the shooting and wondered what that was all about. So, he waited until the shooting stopped and rode around to the back of the house behind Mark.

"Hi, there! I heard you shooting, so I wanted to check to see what was going on."

Mark said, "I'm just starting to learn how to shoot."

The man said, "Can I look at your equipment?"

"Sure," Mark answered.

The man got down off his horse and looked at Mark's gun and holster. He told Mark, "Sorry, guy, but you have the wrong type of holster. It must be cut low in the front allowing you to get the gun out of the holster faster. When you practice with drawing from your holster, pull your hand straight up and out; be sure to lock your eyes on whatever you're shooting at, regardless whether you are standing straight or sideways."

Mark said to the stranger, "Thank you so much. My name is Mark and you are?"

"Just call me Doc."

"Are you a doctor?"

"No," replied the man. "I'm just a traveler and a gambler." And then he left.

A week had gone by and Mark was out in his backyard practicing everyday again. Doc showed up and said, "How you doing?"

Mark replied, "Not so good, but I can't seem to pull my gun out of the holster and hit anything."

Doc handed Mark a piece of rock about the size of a baseball and told him to throw it up in the air as high as he could. When he threw it, Doc pulled his gun and hit the rock twice before it hit the ground. Mark was totally amazed.

"Doc! How did you do that?"

"First, walk up close to your target to where you can hit it. Then, with each shot, back a little farther away. You must visualize in your mind, like a pyramid from your eyes to the target, and from your holster to the target. As you back away on each shot, be sure you hit the target. Keep practicing and it will come to you. Remember one thing, when you get good, never pull your gun unless you intend to use it. You're not going to, are you?"

Mark answered, "No."

Doc had heard the story about Mark's parents being killed by some renegade Mexicans, so he knew in his mind just what Mark was up to, and wanted to help him to get prepared. Doc said his goodbye and left.

Fred had gone by to check on his cattle in the upper field and heard Mark shooting, so he didn't stop to bother him, but was very concerned about what Mark was doing. When Fred arrived back home, he talked to his wife Tina and told her about his concern for Mark.

"I don't think he bought a gun for his own protection. I believe somehow he is planning revenge for his mom and dad. I sure hope not because he may get himself killed!"

Tina asked Fred, "Have you talked to Josh about this? Maybe he could have a nice talk with Mark and help change his mind about him taking revenge."

"Yes, Tina. I have talked to Josh about Mark's behavior, but Josh said he had already warned Mark that if he commits a felony crime, he could also be arrested and put in jail. Josh says he will keep an eye on Mark while he is stationed here, but there is nothing more he can do. I don't think Mark is going to wait to see if those Mexican guys will come back after him. I think when he gets good with a gun, he is going after them."

That Monday morning, Mark went to see Mr. Horan about getting his job back. Mr. Horan told Mark he only had one job open and that's the job his dad had been doing. He asked Mark if he thought he could do that.

Mark replied, "Yes, sir. My dad taught me how ten years ago."

Mr. Horan said he should start the next day at 7 a.m.

Mark arrived at work at 6:45, and looked around for his dad's tools but did not find any. He was a little upset about this, so he waited until Mr. Horan came in, then asked him where his dad's tools were.

Mr. Horan told Mark, I had put them under lock and key in the storage bin because I did not want anyone to use them. Those tools should be yours anyway, so if you would like to use them, I will get them."

Mark answered, "I would like to use them now. Thanks."

Mark had agreed with Mr. Horan to work four days a week, 10 hours a day. He needed his paycheck to sustain himself living alone, and he needed the money to buy bullets and casings for his gun and rifle. Mark had avoided seeing his best friend Charlie and didn't understand why Charlie had not looked him up, knowing he was back working for Mr. Horan. What he didn't know that Charlie and his wife Marlyn had discussed this matter together and decided that it would be better to not see Mark now in his current state of mind and with his strange actions.

During these summer hot months, Mark left his horse Diamond at the Eclipse Livery Stable with Big John Keefer, the Blacksmith and stable caretaker. He liked Mark, and when he was not busy, he would brush Diamond, then wet him with water. Mark and Mr. Keefer became very good friends and Mark knew he could trust him with everything including his secret of being able to identify the Mexicans that killed his parents. Mark never told his friend Josh that he could still draw a picture to help in trying to locate them. However, he did draw each man's picture on an 8" by 10" paper that his dad had got for him, and he gave the three pictures to his friend Mr. Keefer.

Mark told him, "If any of these guys come here, please let me know. I want to kill them.

Mr. Keefer said, "If anyone shows here, I have a young boy that I can have watch the stable while I come to see you."

Mark was doing well on his job to please Mr. Horan, not asking for favors or time off his job. However, he would sometimes develop a late afternoon headache, so he would grab about 6 grams of cannabis and sit for a few minutes, and it usually would let up, sometimes even go away. When Mark got out of work each day, he would walk to the stable, visit Mr. Keefer for a while, take Diamond, and head for home. Mark was unaware that he was being watched each day by not only his Ranger buddy Josh, but also by his dad's friend Fred and Jack Reilly, the local policeman, all being concerned that Mark would someday get into a gun fight with someone and get hurt.

Mark would go home, set up his targets in the backyard and practice with his pistol for an hour every day. At night, he would ride into Denison and look around to see if any Mexicans where hanging out in the local bars. Then about 10p.m., he would go home so he could get up for work the next day. This went on for about three months. In the meantime, Mark was getting very fast and very good with his gun. He could hit the target every time, right where he wanted to.

One day after work, Mark found Texas Ranger Joshua at his house waiting for him to come home.

Josh said to Mark, "I need to have a talk with you, Mark, about the pictures you drew of the killers and gave to the blacksmith. You had told me you couldn't draw anymore since the killing happened. I could arrest you for holding evidence in a murder case, and you could be put in jail."

"Go ahead! Do it!"

Josh said, "No. I just want you to draw the three pictures you gave to Mr. Keefer."

Mark agreed he would draw the pictures of the three Mexicans that killed his Parents and give them to Josh to help him with his investigation.

Josh said, "I want them by tomorrow."

"I'll leave them at Officer Reilly's office tomorrow after work."

Josh said, "I don't want you to say anything to anybody about this."

Mark asked, "Josh, how you got Mr. Keefer to show you the pictures?"

"I saw the pictures lying on the desk in the office, so I talked to him and finally told me you gave them to him after I told him I could arrest him for withholding information in a murder case."

Mark spent that evening drawing the pictures for Josh but they were not exactly as the ones he gave to Mr. Keefer, trying to make it easy for Josh to find them and arrest them before he found them to kill them.

The next morning, when Mark rode in to stable Diamond before he went to work, he talked to Mr. Keefer about the pictures. Mr. Keefer apologized to Mark stating he made a mistake. He had been looking at them and laid them down on the desk to go stable a horse that had just come in, and The Texas Ranger came in and walked into the office and had seen the pictures. He had known who had drawn them. Mark left and went to work knowing that Josh was going to come see him that night when he got home. He wanted to discuss the pictures with him. Mark decided that he would tell Josh the truth. Josh being a long-time friend and a Texas Ranger, might understand much better why he wanted to hide the identity of these men.

Mark left work at about 3:30 that afternoon, picked up Diamond at the stable, and rode home. Yes, Josh was there with Fred, and they both wanted to talk to him. This made Mark a little uncomfortable. He didn't want to talk to both of them, but he tried to stay cool and take his time answering questions.

Fred said to Mark, "You know we have been not just

friends, but like family, and you will always be part of our family. I want you to know we are here to love and support you, and help you in any way we can."

"Yes, I know, but my Mom and Dad are dead. Someone has to pay for that."

Josh spoke up and said to Mark, "We have been friends since we were little kids. I had troubles too. I had my own thinking that my parents loved my sister more than me. You know I got into a lot of trouble and left home. I met a Texas Ranger who had the same problems as I did. He had two sisters and got in lots of trouble. He helped straighten me out and got me into the Rangers. Now, he's my best friend. So, never get the idea that your friends will not help because they always will."

Mark replied to Josh, "Yes, we have been buddies for a long time, but how would you feel if someone killed your parents? What would you do? And don't say just let family handle it, or the police departments."

Josh answered, "I believe how you feel and I agree, but it's the responsibility of law officers to track down and put them in jail unless they resist then we have to kill them. Otherwise, we must use due process of the law in murder cases. But for you to pursue this on your own is crazy! You yourself could get killed or be arrested for murder the same as they will be when caught."

Mark made no reply to Josh concerning what his intentions were to be from that day on. He just handed the drawings over to Josh and said nothing more. Then, both Fred and Josh had noticed that Mark had drawings of pictures all over the walls in the kitchen and living room of his mom and dad.

"I'm telling you, dad, I'm really concerned as to what Mark is going to do."

"I know, Josh. We also are. Even the guys he works with say he acts strange at times, and does not really talk to anybody, not even his old buddy Charlie."

Josh replied to his dad, "Yes, I did see that. What I'm going to do is to get these pictures out today to Ranger Headquarters. They will get copies out to all Rangers in Texas. Hopefully, we can get them soon before Mark decides to go hunt for them."

The next morning, Mark left for work at 6:00 a.m. He wanted to see and talk to his friend Big John Keefer, the stable boss, and leave Diamond for the day.

When he arrived, Big John was there, and said, "I'm glad you came in today. I wanted to tell you what happened last night. I had a couple of Mexican guys stop here. They wanted their horses shod. So, I had the shoes they needed, and while I was working, I noticed them looking at the pictures of yours that I hung on the wall outside the office. I asked them if they knew any of these guys, but denied they knew any of them. They talked in Spanish to themselves then acted strangely. This sounded very strange to me, so after I finished my job, I decided to ride around town to see if these Mexicans were hanging out in one of the bars. Sure enough, they were in Boland's saloon at the bar. They knew me, so I didn't go in, but I saw their horses tied in front of the Dennison Hotel. They must be still here."

Mark said, "Please, Big John; don't say anything to anyone. I will be down later after work to get Diamond, then look around town. If they are still here, I'll find them.

If not, they may go down to Sherman to one of their bars. I will stop and see you before I go hunting. If you hear anything about them, let me know."

After work, Mark went home to grab his gun. He went into the backyard for a half hour to practice. He then took his gun apart and cleaned it like it was brand new. Like his friend Doc had told him, always keep your gun clean and never pull your gun out of the holster unless you intend to use it. Mark put on his dark clothing, so it was not so easy to spot after dark. He rode back into Denison and stopped at the stable.

Big John said, "I have some information for you. Those guys that were here are, or were, members of the William Quant's gang. They are very dangerous and don't care who they kill. They usually go into a town for a couple days, get drunk, rape women, and steal what they want, then leave."

Mark asked, "Did either of these guys look like any one of the pictures?"

"No," replied Big John. "But they travel in pairs, so if they get into a gun fight, they always have two against one. That's how they always win, so be careful out there."

"Thank you, Big John. I will; but I must go out and look around."

Checking out the local bars, Mark saw some Mexicans in Chichet saloon. He decided that he would go in for a drink of sarsaparilla, and see if he could find the one who speaks English. The bartender could speak both Spanish and English. As Mark entered the bar, all the Mexican started laughing. They had never seen anyone dressed like Mark with a gun on and an Amish-style straw hat. Mark walked down to the end of the bar and ordered a drink. The Mexican standing next to him could speak English, so he asked Mark if he was a gunslinger. Mark replied that he wasn't.

The Mexican said, "You look like a gunslinger."

"No. I am not a gunslinger." Mark looked around in the bar, but saw no one he knew would help him with information.

Two Mexican guys standing next to him got up and left. Mark finished his drink and walked out of the bar going to mount Diamond and have a look around at other bars. Suddenly, he heard a Mexican yell to him

"Hey, Gunslinger! Are you fast?"

Mark looked at him, and it was the same guy that had been in the bar.

Mark answered, "Mister, I don't want to hurt you. You are not the person I am looking for."

"Sorry, then I must hurt you," answered the Mexican and drew his gun.

Before he had cleared his holster, Mark had shot him through the arm. At the same time, another gun rang out, and a Mexican standing on a porch fell over dead in the road. Mark looked around and he saw Doc standing on the deck with his gun still smoking in his hand. Doc waved to Mark to tell him to get out of town. Police Officer Reilly showed up just in time to see the whole thing happen. He also waved to Mark telling him to get out of town, and he yelled to him saying he would be out to see him the next day.

Chapter 15

Mark left Denison and went home. Now, he wondered if the Mexicans would come in the middle of the night after him. So, he slept in the living room on the couch with his gun and rifle next to him. It turned out to be a quiet night.

The next morning, Officer Reilly showed up to talk to Mark. Josh was not around because he had been sent out of town on business, so he knew nothing about this. Officer Reilly asked Mark what had happened to cause a gun fight. Mark then explained how he went to the bar to try to get information on the three guys he was looking for, but the Mexicans had only laughed at him and talked mostly in Spanish. He told Reilly about the one Mexican that did talk to him asking him if he were a gun-slinger.

"I told him no, but when I left the bar after him, he was waiting for me in the street. He wanted to kill me."

Officer Reilly said, "Yes, I know. The Mexican talked to me after you had gone. He had admitted he was the fault of the gun fight. He also told me that you were the fastest guy with a gun that he had ever seen, and he was the only one hurt. If I would let them go, they would get out of town tonight and not come back. Well, they left last night. They all must have been part of one gang because they all left at once."

Mark didn't feel well. He could not wait until Officer Reilly left. He went to the kitchen to get his medicine and found he had nothing left but aspirin; his cannabis were gone.

It was Saturday morning and he knew he needed to get help before his headache got worse. So, he took three aspirin and went to the barn to get Diamond. He started getting dizzy but managed to get the saddle on Diamond. He mounted Diamond and started riding toward town slowly. Mark leaned forward in his saddle and told his horse go to Doctor Bailey's. He knew he was going to pass out before they reached Denison. He sure did about half way there. Mark's horse, Diamond, knew he did by the way he was sitting in the saddle. So, Diamond walked slowly right into Denison and stopped right in front of the store where Doctor Bailey's office was. People in front of the store saw Mark hanging onto the saddle and ran to get Doc Bailey. He and a Mexican man helped get Mark down off the horse and into his office.

Mark was having a flashback of his parents being killed while being passed out. Doc Bailey gave him a shot to calm him down. After about a half hour, he came to and didn't even know where he was. Doc Bailey questioned Mark about what had happened. He told him that he ran out of medicine. Doctor Bailey examined Mark, checking for bumps or lumps on top of his head, but found nothing.

Doc said, "Your problem appears to be getting worse. What I would like you to do is to sign yourself into Saint Vincent's hospital for further examination. They have recently acquired a new machine they call an x-ray machine, and it was invented in 1895. It will allow Doctor James to look inside your head to see if you have a tumor."

Mark asked Doctor Bailey if he could give him some more medicine and postpone the hospital visit for a while, saying he had some important things to do.

Doc Bailey said, "I will give you medicine to last you for 30 days, then I want you into the hospital. Is that agreeable?"

Mark replied that it was. His horse was tied to the hitching post in front of the store when he left doc's office. Mark got on his horse and rode over to the Eclipse Livery Stable to see his good friend Big John Keefer, to tell him what was going on, and to see if John had obtained any information as to the location of the men he was after.

John told Mark that there had been a rider that stopped to get his horse shod the other day. He was looking at the posters on the wall and said he had seen two of those men in a bar near Dallas, Texas.

Mark asked John, "Did you know the man?"

John answered, "No, but he had been there before, about a year ago. He gets his horse shod and moves on. I think he has a relative somewhere up in New York."

"Did he look or speak like he was of Spanish descent?"

"No, he was not a Mexican, and did not even look like one."

Mark thanked John for the information and left. Mark rested for the weekend, then went into work on Monday morning. He waited for Mr. Horan to come in, then he went to his office to ask to speak with him. He then asked Mr. Horan if he could have a little time off work.

"How long?" asked Mr. Horan.

"About ten days."

"Okay, you have it starting tomorrow. I want you back here on the 11th day. Is that clear?"

"Yes," Mark answered.

After leaving his job, Mark had gone to Hayes Gentleman's Clothing Store, and bought a white cowboy hat. He was going to wear it on his trip to Dallas tomorrow. He didn't want to go wearing an Amish style straw hat that could also start a fight. He decided to take the hat in his duffel bag because if he found the Mexicans he was looking for, he would put it on as he killed them.

Mark had become very bitter since the murder of his parents and his outward personality had become poor. He was determined he would find these men himself and kill them with no mercy at all. He left for Dallas, Texas that very next morning. He was not sure where he was going to Dallas, but he would search, section by section, in and around Dallas until he could get a lead on where the Mexican families were located.

Mark arrived in Dallas, the northeast corner of Coppell County the next morning. He was dressed in blue jeans, a shirt, cowboy boots, and his cowboy hat so that it would appear he was just a cowboy riding through that area. As he rode through little hamlets in that County, he did notice there were several little bars and Saloons down the main streets, a good place to start looking at night. He stopped at a blacksmith shop to have Diamond's right front foot looked at, as it was bleeding a little. The blacksmith's name was Charlie Gillison.

Mr. Gillison was a local resident that lived in that area for several years. He found a small nail in Diamond's foot and removed it. Later in conversation with Mr. Gillison, Mark began to feel comfortable talking with him. He asked him if he spoke Spanish.

Mr. Gillison said he did. "Anything I can help you with?"

Mark decided to try to show his three drawings to see what would happen. Mr. Gillison looked at them and said to Mark, "Yes! These guys have been here! The first two are brothers and the third guy is a cousin."

"Do you know their names or where they live?"

"Sorry I can't help you there. Only see them a couple times a year. I can give you their names, but I have no idea where they live. The brothers are Paloma and Pastora Binito. The third guy here, I'm not quite sure, but I think his name was Antonio Bernardo. What are you looking for these guys for?"

"Just a little business to handle with them."

"A little tip, these guys are bad news. Be careful. They have been in the Dallas jail several times, arrested by the Dallas Police and the County Sheriff's Department according to the paper; once for murder, but were never convicted of that crime."

Mark thanked Mr. Gillison for the information and suggested he go to the Sheriff Department to get information as to where they live. He did not want to arouse the police on what he was doing there looking for those guys, so he decided he would stay overnight at the local hotel, then he could scout around the town at that evening to see who showed up at the local bars and saloons.

That night was pretty quiet. Mark started walking up and down the street looking in the doors and windows of the saloons to see who might be there, but to no available. Only the local drunkards were in the bars.

When Mark left to go to Dallas, he told no one where he was going, not even his boss. Fred and Tina were very concerned, especially with his health problems. They inquired around Denison from people that knew Mark. They asked at work, and Mr. Horan told them Mark had asked for time off and he had given him ten days that was all he could tell them. They inquired at doctor Bailey's, and was told that Mark had refused to go to the hospital for tests for the next 30 days and he hadn't said why.

"I gave him a thirty-day supply of medication for those headaches. That's all I could do."

Charlie and Marlyn were looking for Mark also. They had gone to his house to see if he had left a note to where he was going. They knew if he found any information about those Mexicans, he would go after them even if he got killed. Joshua, the Texas Ranger, had been reassigned and was out of the area. They had no idea where he was. Charlie knew Mark was good friends with Mr. Keefer, and went to ask him if he knew anything. Keefer told him he might have gone to Dallas. He said he was going on vacation. Thought he might go to Dallas.

Charlie said to Mr. Keefer," Dallas is a large city. Did he say where in Dallas he was going?"

Keefer answered that all he said was Dallas.

Charlie said, "Dallas is a large city with several districts around the city, would not even know where to begin to look for him."

Mr. Keefer replied, "If you are going looking for him I might suggest you check with the City Police and the County Sheriff's Department. They may be able to help you find him."

Charlie decided he would talk this over with wife Marlyn before he made any decisions to make the trip to Dallas looking for him.

Marlyn said to Charlie, "We both know why he went to Dallas. Somehow, he found out the men who killed his parents are somewhere in that Dallas area, and he's going to go after them. Let's just wait for the ten days and see if he comes home."

Charlie agreed.

Fred had had a chance to sell all three of John's horses that he was taking care of and keeping in his barn for Mark, but he would not sell them until Mark told him he could. Mark loves those horses because they were his dad's and mom's. He decided he would stay in that area for another three days, thinking if he made a few friends there he might be able to find out where these guys were living.

Mark found a local stable to keep his horse in, feed him, and take care of him for a couple of days. Mark did not realize how large the Dallas city was, with a population at that time of 38,000 people and the largest police force in the United States. He knew at that time that if he could not get a lead on these guys, it would be almost impossible to find them. And yet, he did not want to go to the police to try to get information, because they would certainly ask questions and make him a suspect if there were any recent murders in the area he was staying, because he was a total stranger.

The next day, Mark decided he would go get Diamond and take a two or three mile ride west of the village where he was staying. Maybe he would get lucky and find someone that might be able to tell him something that would help. But there were many Mexican families along this route and they did not appear very friendly, so he returned to the village and just hung out hoping to talk to people.

Mark put Diamond back in the stable and then walked down the street. He stopped in front of the local store on Main Street and sat on one of the benches in front of the store. It was Friday and nothing much was going on during the day. While he was sitting there, the store manager came out of the store to have a smoke. He sat down beside Mark.

"Hey, young man. Can I ask you a question?"

Mark said sure.

"I see you're new in town. Are you a gunslinger?"

Mark replied, "No, why do you ask that question?"

"I noticed your gun and a low-cut holster. Have you killed anybody?"

"No," replied Mark. "Not yet."

"If you are a gunman, you must go to the Dallas Police Department, and register your gun. It's a law."

Mark answered, "Yes, the next time I get down in the city, I'll do that."

He had no idea of doing that. He was not going to register his gun with the police when he was planning to kill a couple of guys. Mark hung around for a while. A couple of young ladies smiled at him as they entered the store, but he was not interested in women. He just wanted to find the Mexicans, kill them and go home. Mark decided, after sitting on that store bench for a while, he would go into a couple of saloons and have a drink. He only drank sarsaparilla, but he wanted to try to get to know the bartenders; maybe they might be able to discuss their bar and table activities.

The bartenders were friendly, but because Mark was new in town, they asked more questions than information they were willing to give out. Like, "Hi! Where are you from? What kind of work do you do? Are you here to buy something?"

Mark answered, "No, I'm on vacation; just passing through, staying a few days here and there."

"Do you have family living down here in Dallas?"

"No one," replied Mark.

While visiting in the second bar that Mark went into, a couple of Mexican men came in for a drink and started talking in Spanish with the bartender, and the bartender talked back to them in Spanish. Mark noticed they were looking at him, so, he got up and left, went back to his room to rest for a while because he was going to scout out the bars and saloons in that area after 9 p.m. He decided he would stay there through Sunday night and keep watching.

If the three Mexicans he was looking for didn't show up, he would move on to a different area around the City of Dallas. Mark knew it would take him three to four days to get back to Denison from the Dallas area. However, he was determined he was not going to leave until he found these guys. He did pack enough medication to take that would last for the next 20 days, and money that he had saved for this trip.

Now came Saturday morning. Mark woke up early with a slight headache so he took a little of his cannabis and an aspirin, and laid on the bed for a while. Finally, the pain and headache stopped. He got dressed, went down to the bar in the hotel for breakfast, and sat at a little table for two. Four local men came in for breakfast and sat at the round table next to him. They all started talking about their jobs and what was going on around that area.

One of the men said, "Hey, did you see in the paper that the County Sheriffs arrested Antonio Bernardo?"

"No! What happened?"

"According to the article, he shot an unarmed man and stole his horse. They may hang him. He sure will get a death sentence."

This shocked Mark knowing he was one of the men he was after. Mark said nothing to the four men. He did not want to ask any questions of them or later be connected in any way with them.

Chapter 16

After leaving the bar, Mark walked up to the stable to see Diamond and talk with Mr. Gillison about what he had heard while having breakfast. He asked Mr. Gillison if he had read the Dallas paper and the article about Antonio Bernardo.

"No, I have not seen the paper recently," replied Mr. Gillison. "What's happening?"

Mark told Mr. Gillison what he had heard. Mr. Gillison asked if that wasn't one of the guys he was looking for. Mark answered yes.

Mr. Gillison asked, "Why?"

Mark answered, "I will tell you if you promise to tell no one."

Mr. Gillison assured Mark he would say nothing to anyone ever. So, he told Gillison, "They shot and killed my mom and dad. Now, I'm going to kill them."

"Please be very careful. These are bad men. They don't care about anyone, not even their own relatives."

"Thanks for your concern for me, but now it's them or me."

Mark asked Mr. Gillison if his horse was in good shape and ready to go.

Gillison Replied, "Yes, he is. I checked his feet and legs and he's ready to go."

"Good. I thank you for your service. I want to pay you your stable cost now and for each one day in advance, in case I have to leave this area fast." He paid for three days and left.

Saturday morning was a little busy in this village. People were out shopping buying their groceries and shopping in the surrounding department stores. Mark decided to park himself on a park bench in front of one of the stores, just to observe the action going on, while watching whoever rode by, hoping it would be one of the Mexicans he was looking for. No luck that morning, so he decided he would go back to his room at the hotel and rest for a while. He did not want to overdo it and wind up with one of his headaches, then not be able to go out in the street later.

The Hotel Dallas annex had a nice bar and dinner dining area right off the lobby entrance. Mark woke from his nap about 6:00 p.m., and was a little hungry. He strapped on his gun and went to the dining area. After dinner at about 7:00 p.m., he went back to his favorite park bench. Activities had slowed down a lot since the morning activities, so there was not much going on in the street. At about 8:30 p.m., two men on horses came riding slowly down the street. Mark was watching them as they stopped and entered one of the local saloons. He could tell it was the two brothers he was looking for. He waited for a while, then walked down the street and looked in the window and saw the two Mexicans sitting at the bar. He confirmed they were the guys he was looking for. Mark saw a young boy about 15 or 16 years old coming down the street and asked him to go into the bar and asked for Paloma and Pastora. Tell them there is a man outside who wants to talk to them. The kid's name was James Baker, a local boy.

The went into the saloon entrance and yelled out, "Paloma and Pastora! A man outside wants to talk to you guys!"

Paloma asked, "Who told you our names?"

Baker answered, "The man outside did. He gave me a five-dollar bill just to come in here and tell you he wants to talk to you both... now."

Paloma got off his bar stool, walked over to the door, looked out and saw Mark standing in the street. He turned around and said to his brother Pastora, "I have never seen this guy. I don't know who he is."

Pastora asked if he was wearing a badge.

"No, not that I can see."

"Well, come back here and finish your beer. Then, we will go out together and see what this guy wants."

Mark waited for them to come out of the bar into the street. It was getting dark but it was a bright moonlit night. While Mark was waiting for the men to come out into the street, he took off his cowboy hat, put on his Amish style straw hat, and put his cowboy hat on the saddle horn of Diamond, standing at the hitching post next to Mark.

The two men walked out of the bar to the middle of the street and asked, "What you want? You want to get killed?"

Mark replied, "No, I came here to kill you, men. Remember the man and woman you shot and killed in North Denison? They we my parents. Now, I'm going to kill you!"

The Mexicans looked at each other and both drew their pistols at the same time. But not good enough. Mark drew his gun and shot two shots killing them both. They were dead before they even hit the ground. The people standing on the street were quiet and never said a word to Mark. Before he killed them, the bartender said he would call the undertaker and the police. Mark just turn around, mounted Diamond and started out of town. He knew that he was 69 miles away from Denison, and it would take him three days to get home. Since it was a nice bright moonlit night, Mark decided he would ride most of the night or until he felt tired, then look for cover and stop somewhere.

The next morning, the county Sheriff with two men showed up and started to question people who had seen what happened. People who had been on the street all said they heard Mark say they were the ones who shot and killed his parents, and he was there to kill them. They all said they saw the men draw their guns, but Mark was much faster. The undertaker told the Sheriff that one man was shot right through the middle of the heart, and the other right between the eyes. The Sheriff asked what the shooter's name was, but they didn't know.

The blacksmith said all he knew was his first name, that it was Mark, but no last name. Sheriff asked where he was from.

Gillison answered, "I didn't know. He had never told

me, and I didn't ask."

The Sheriff said, "We have their cousin in jail. Maybe he can tell us where we can find him."

Back at the office, the Sheriff contacted the Dallas Police Chief. He had told the sheriff a couple of months ago that a Texas Ranger had come in looking for some information on those guys. He told us he was from Denison, Texas, this was where that murder had happened. The Ranger's name was Joshua Martin.

Mark rode all night and made two stops on his way home; first at Lowry Crossings, then at South Savoy. Both were room and board houses. He slept days and rode at night as it was starting to get dark because it was easier on Diamond than riding all day in the hot sun.

On the third night, he had arrived home, put his horse Diamond in the barn where it was cool. Mark went into the house took his gun belt off and hung it on a ten-penny nail between the pictures of his Mom and Dad that he had drawn on poster paper; vowed to never to put that belt or gun on again. He was very tired and did not sleep well on his trip home. He laid on his bed and had some mixed emotions about what he had done. He remembered what his buddy Texas Ranger Josh had said – that this would also make him a murderer. He slept for about ten hours, and when he awoke, someone was knocking at his door. It was Fred and Tina.

Fred asked, "Where have you been? We have been looking for you for three days!"

"I took a little vacation to Dallas. I wanted to see how the big city life was."

"Well, we were quite worried, so we are happy to see you back."

Mark did not tell them anything about what happened in Dallas. Fred and Tina were visiting for a while with Mark, when all of a sudden, Mark fell out of his chair to the floor passed out. Fred saw Mark's duffel bag on the counter and found some cannabis and pain pill in the pocket. He told Tina to get a glass of water to see if they could get him to take some. They did manage to get him to take a little. After about fifteen minutes, Mark came to with a big headache.

Tina said, "Lucky we brought the wagon instead of riding here. We'd better get him down to Doctor Bailey's office on our wagon."

"Yes, you're right," said Fred.

He asked Mark if he could stand up and walk.

Mark answered, "Yes, I'm okay."

Fred told Tina to take a couple blankets off the bed, and to put them on the wagon for Mark to lie on. They traveled very slowly to Denison to Doctor Bailey's office. When they arrived, Tina went into the office to explain what had happened.

Doctor Bailey came out to the wagon, checked Mark over, and said, "Keep him right on the wagon. This has gone far enough. I want you to take him over to Saint Vincent's Hospital now!"

When arriving at the Hospital, Doctor George Rupert came out to the wagon to look at Mark. He turned and said to Fred and Tina to go sign him in.

"We will get a stretcher and put him in examination room. We had now a new machine called X-Ray, and they would be able to see into Mark's brain to try to detect what's going on. This would take about a week after the X-rays are taken because they must be sent out to be developed and read, then returned back to here, at the hospital. Anything abnormal happening in Mark's brain, we'll be able to see and understand," Doctor Rupert informed Fred and Tina.

Fred and Tina left the hospital only to return to visit with Mark during visiting hours three day later. Mark had been in the intensive care unit in the hospital and had recovered nicely and wanted to go home. But he was told he could not go home until the X-Rays came back. He suspected there was a serious problem, so he decided to talk to Fred about his parent's home. Mark asked Fred to go ahead and sell the house, but begged not to sell Diamond because he love that horse so much.

Fred answered, "Don't worry. I would never even think of selling your horse."

Mark added, "Please use my money to pay the hospital bills."

Fred assured him that he definitely would. Tina told Mark that Charlie and Marlyn would be there to see him soon, and they have something special to tell him. The next day, Joshua Texas Ranger showed up, and this made Mark happy.

Joshua then told Mark, "Boy! You are a real hero in the Dallas area! Everybody, even the police, are happy these men are gone. They were real bad men. So, thank you."

Mark smiled and said, "Yes, I'm glad it's over. Please do me a favor. Go to my parent's house. On the living room wall, take down the pictures of them and my holster and gun between them. Just get that done before the house is sold."

Josh assured Mark that he would take care of it.

That afternoon, Charlie and Marlyn came to visit.

Charlie said, "Guess what? We have a surprise for you! Marlyn is pregnant! I'm going to be a father! We have decided if it's a boy, we are going to name him Mark, and if its girl, Markie."

Mark smiled and held Marlyn's hand as he had always loved her, and Charlie was his buddy.

That night of October 10th, 1905, at 9:45 p.m., at age 32, Mark died of a quick and sudden brain hemorrhage.

The End

*This book has been researched and written
in its entirety by:*

Edward A. Congdon

www.ingramcontent.com/pod-product-compliance
Lightning Source LLC
Chambersburg PA
CBHW061307210726
48293CB00003B/1149